Thanksgiving
by Mary R. Arno

© Copyright 2014 Mary R. Arno

ISBN 978-1-63393-157-2

Published by

◄ köehlerbooks ™

210 60th Street
Virginia Beach, VA 23451
212-574-7939
www.koehlerbooks.com

THANKSGIVING

mary r. arno

VIRGINIA BEACH
CAPE CHARLES

For Phil,
who never doubted;
and Sarah, Warren, Joe and Anna,
always in my heart.

God, for the gladness here where the sun is shining at evening
on the weeds at the river,
Our prayer of thanks . . .

For the break of the game and the first
play and the last,
Our prayer of thanks.

—Carl Sandburg

CHAPTER ONE

kenner

ARKANSAS WAS THE LAST street for as far as you could
see in the newest, barest western end of Kenner, Louisiana.
The residential grid where Peg Hennessy grew up was perfectly
symmetrical—every lot fifty feet across, one hundred feet back.
Twenty-four houses on a block, twelve on each side. A smooth
white concrete ribbon of a street, no lumpy bricks with tree roots
that could trip a kid off her bike. Of course, a few trees would
be nice . . .

*Buzz, buzz, chop, chop, mow, mow. Pile drivers pound
thirty-foot logs into the ground on the next block of Arkansas.
Then the cement mixers spawn neat, identical rectangular
slabs, each with a driveway extending like the tail of an
amoeba. Sturdy foundations prove New Greenlawn Terrace
is quality—at least that's what Daddy says. These rows of
houses along alphabetically ordered state-named streets will
last. They won't sink into the marshy mud or end up leaning
and tottering into a wobbly middle age like the tiny, wooden
houses in Old Greenlawn. No, this is 1965, and Daddy says
New Greenlawn is built for the ages.*

Houses were springing up, but the neighborhood still had
plenty of wilderness to play in. If you could get through the

tall grass behind the Hennessys' fence, you could walk from their backyard to Lake Pontchartrain and into St. Charles Parish without seeing another house or street. The kids in the neighborhood called it the Weeds back there. There were thorny bushes of wild blackberries, which they sometimes picked. But they usually ate most of them before they got home. Also, there was the Canal, which was actually a ditch that emptied into Lake Pontchartrain.

The kids in my family are allowed to play in the Weeds, but we aren't supposed to go near the Canal. My mother says we could drown. But I am eleven, and I know that drowning is pretty unlikely since the Canal is less than a foot deep. Of course, you could sink in the mud.

I don't like going back there much because it stinks, but my four little brothers and their friends play there a lot. Sometimes we come back smelling awful, and Mama hoses us off before she lets us inside.

People in Kenner are different. Mama says some of them are not well bred. Some of them say "ain't" and one boy says "nigger." Also some of them have funny accents, and there are a lot of Protestants, mostly Baptist. In the summer, they go for Bible lessons. They call it Vacation Babble School, which sounds pretty funny.

Some of the families had come from places farther away than New Orleans. Emmaline Mackey, for example. She was almost two years older than Peg, but only one grade ahead because they started school later where she comes from. Also, her family moved a lot.

Emmaline likes to go back in the Weeds and doesn't mind the smell. We look for rocks and smash them open with a hammer to see if the insides sparkle. We take picnics so we don't have to come in for lunch. Mama always makes me a bologna sandwich or peanut butter. Emmaline fixes her own. Once she made a Bosco sandwich.

* * * *

Looking back on it, Peg realized that Emmaline knew all kinds of grown-up stuff, a lot more than Peg, which could be embarrassing. Sometimes Peg tried to pretend she knew, like when Emmaline talked about French-kissing with Merle and asked Peg if her father ever French-kissed her. Peg was horrified and couldn't think of what to say.

"Why do you call your daddy Merle?" she asked.

"He's not my daddy."

The girls had stayed out too long and Miss Ruby, Emmaline's mother, was pretty mad. When they had got back to where the street ended in the Weeds, they could hear Miss Ruby yelling out of the kitchen window. "Emmaline, Emmaline! Git in here, girl!"

Emmaline looked a little scared. "You come in, Peg," she said over her shoulder as she ran ahead. "Then she won't hit me."

Peg wasn't too crazy about facing an angry Miss Ruby. Even worse were Emmaline's older brother, Harry, and his friends, who mostly didn't wear shirts or go to school. They just worked on the cars and motorcycles parked in their driveway. Definitely not well bred, Peg thought. But Peg wasn't a chicken, so she followed Emmaline. When she got to the door, Miss Ruby was holding Emmaline by the arm and whispering in her ear in a kind of hiss.

"Girl, you was supposed to be washing—Oh, hi, Peg." She let go of Emmaline. Bright red stripes from her fingers circled Emmaline's upper arm. "Well, give your friend something to drank." Miss Ruby walked away. When she opened the door to the back bedroom, Peg could hear men talking.

"You want some coffee?" Emmaline asked.

"You're allowed to have coffee?"

"Oh sure, I can even make it." Emmaline took the coffee pot over to the faucet, ducking below the brown swags of flypaper speckled with dead insects draped over the sink. She ran water over the used grounds, then put the pot on the stove and lit the burner. Blue gas flickers surrounded the blackened bottom of the tin pot. Emmaline rubbed her arm, but Miss Ruby's finger marks didn't go away. After a couple of minutes, she got a dishtowel, turned off the burner, lifted the pot, and poured two cups. It didn't look like coffee. It looked too light even for tea. Emmaline put milk from the carton into both cups and then heaped in three spoons of sugar. Then she stuck the wet spoon back in the sugar bowl and passed it over to Peg. Peg shook a spoonful into her cup, took one sip, and almost spit it back.

"I guess I got to do the wash," Emmaline said. "You don't have to stay."

"I can help."

"Okay." Emmaline gulped the rest of her coffee and went to the back of the house. "I'll get the clothes and stuff."

Peg dumped her coffee in the sink and rinsed both cups. "I'll wait outside."

The washing machine sat under the carport, since their laundry room was filled with tires, oilcans, and other grease-covered objects. Emmaline crammed an armload of shirts and pants into the washer and dumped some detergent on top without even separating the whites. She started the machine.

"Well, we got a few minutes," she said. "Want a smoke?" She pulled an open pack of Chesterfields from her pocket. "I found 'em in Harry's shirt," she whispered. "Come on, we can go in the back."

It was afternoon and the melted tar oozing up from the expansion joints in the street made the air smell like burned licorice. Peg's mother was probably napping, which meant the boys and Janie were inside too, but it was best to check. You never knew what tattletales might be around. "I have to go home and get lunch," Peg said. "I'll meet you there."

Sure enough, the boys were sleeping in their bunk beds, and Janie was in the big double bed with Peg's mother. Peg was looking around for something to eat when the doorbell rang. She figured it was Emmaline and ran to open the door before the bell rang again and woke her mother.

A man in a suit stood on the stoop, carrying a briefcase. He smiled like he wanted to sell something. "Is your mother home?" he asked.

"We don't want any," Peg said, and that quick, he grabbed the handle on the screen and stuck his foot into the jamb so she couldn't close the door. Peg backed away from the door. He came inside and shut it and moved into the living room, looking around. He set his briefcase next to the sofa. Peg wished the house weren't so quiet. He walked toward her, backing her into the kitchen.

This is definitely a problem. Mama's main rule is never to talk to strangers, much less let them in the house. If she wakes up right now, she'll be very mad.

In the kitchen, the stranger smiled at Peg. She began to feel more afraid of him than of her mother. She moved ahead of him to block the hallway leading back to the bedrooms.

"I have to use the john," he said, shoving Peg aside as he pushed past into the bathroom. He shut the door and she heard the knob lock turn. Peg wanted to run, but she couldn't leave him in the house with everybody sleeping.

If I wake up Mama, she'll yell and maybe make him mad. Does he have a gun? A knife? Maybe he's going to kill us all. My face feels hot and it is getting hard to breathe. I can feel tears forming. My stomach hurts.

She closed the door to the boys' room, and to her mother's.

Please, God, let him just go to the bathroom and then go away.

Peg waited, watching the kitchen clock. He had been in the bathroom for seven minutes.

I have to do something. He's probably not even a salesman.

She went to his briefcase, lifted out a large binder and opened it. The first page had a list of addresses on Arkansas Street, California Street, Colorado Street.

Good sign. Maybe he really is just a salesman who had to go.

She leafed through the binder, trying to figure out what he was selling.

A knock on the front door. This time, Peg looked out the window before opening. It was Emmaline.

"What's taking you so long?" Emmaline demanded.

Peg held up the binder. "This guy, he's been in the bathroom for ages, and my mother is asleep back there."

"What are you talking about?" Emmaline asked. But when they went into the hall to check, the door was open and the bathroom empty. The hallway was lit only by a triangle of sunlight coming from the open door to Peg's bedroom.

They could hear bedsprings squeaking. Peg peeked around the corner and quickly backed up.

"What?" Emmaline asked.

"He's sitting on my bed and his pants are off."

"In his undershorts?"

"No."

The girls looked at each other. "Let's get him out," Emmaline said.

Peg gulped. "I'll do it," she said. "If I yell, run out the front door before he can get you."

Emmaline picked up the binder. "We'll go together," she said, shoving Peg ahead of her down the hallway.

Peg stopped at the door of her bedroom. The man was sitting on her bedspread with the pink flowers and bows, his knees wide open. His eyes were closed and his face was sweaty. When he heard the girls, he woke up and slapped his thighs shut. "Don't come in," he called out.

Peg started to leave, but Emmaline stepped forward. "Hey, Mr. Pervert," Emmaline said, holding up his binder. She ripped out a page. The man jumped up and tried to grab it, but with his pants around his ankles, he did a little hobble and then tripped.

Emmaline started ripping up the page she'd torn from the binder. "You want anything left of this thing, you better pull up your pants and get your dirty butt out of here," she said. Then she ripped out another page and turned around. Peg followed her down the hallway to the living room.

A minute later, the man was in the living room too, his pants up but his shirt untucked. He yanked the binder from Emmaline and grabbed the torn scraps of paper on the floor. He stuffed everything into his briefcase and held it close to his chest as he went out the front door. They watched him walk very fast to the end of Arkansas and turn toward Williams Boulevard.

They were still watching when the other bedroom door opened. Peg's mother came into the living room, her face pink and creased from the pillowcase. "What's going on, Peg?" she asked. "Is somebody here?"

"Just me and Emmaline, Mama."

"Well, don't wake up the boys," she said, going back in her room and closing the door.

Emmaline and Peg looked at each other. "I can't believe she slept through that," Emmaline said.

"She doesn't like to have her nap disturbed," Peg said. "Like when I got home from school and woke her up to tell her President Kennedy had died, she said not to do that again unless it was Daddy that died."

They went to the kitchen, where Peg made a peanut butter and Sunbeam bread sandwich and wrapped it in wax paper. She took a bottle of Coca-Cola from the refrigerator. Emmaline watched as Peg rearranged the rest of the bottles to disguise the fact that one was missing. She flipped the cap off at the bottle opener by the door, took a sip, and handed the Coke to Emmaline, who took a sip as they headed out the door.

Mosquitos buzzed as they walked to the end of the block and then into the Weeds. Peg slapped at her leg, wishing she had used the bottle of bug spray by the back door. They sat against a weeping willow with a thick canopy of shade. Emmaline lifted a cigarette out of the pack and stuck it in her mouth. She sucked in while the tip of the cigarette lit, then started coughing and dropped the match in the grass. She laughed as Peg jumped up and stamped on it. "Only YOU can prevent weed fires," Emmaline said. Peg laughed too as she took the cigarette from Emmaline. She put it in her mouth and sucked.

It tastes like the car fumes that come up from the hole in the floor of Daddy's '57 Ford. Peg coughed even more than Emmaline had.

"You got to breathe in while the smoke is in your mouth," Emmaline said as she took the cigarette back. Emmaline inhaled again to demonstrate. She didn't cough this time, just closed her eyes and leaned against the tree trunk. After a few seconds, she handed it back. Peg shook her head no.

They sat in the shade while Emmaline finished the cigarette. That's what Peg liked about Emmaline. You didn't have to talk all the time.

Mama says Emmaline's family is common, because, for one thing, Emmaline's little sister Jolene goes around all summer without a shirt on. But I told Mama that doesn't matter since she's only four. Once I heard Mama tell Daddy that Miss Ruby isn't married. But I know that isn't right. Emmaline says Miss Ruby has been married three times. I don't think I'll correct Mama on that one, though.

Mama likes it better when I play with Phyllis Brown, who is in my class at St. Joan of Arc School. But Phyllis doesn't like to read or talk about books, just about what boys she thinks are cute. On the other hand, Emmaline thinks it's silly to pretend to be detectives, which I like to do since I have been reading the Nancy Drew books. Different friends for different things, I figure.

Emmaline blew smoke rings. The air was hot and thick as grillades. From behind the willow, Peg could see the roof of Emmaline's house. She squinted and imagined the long thin willow leaves were ballerinas, swaying in the little ripples of smoke that Emmaline blew. Peg had read that willow leaves were poison.

Daddy joined the civil defense. He says that's so when the Russians invade, Mama and the rest of us can stay at the bomb shelter under city hall while he goes to do whatever the civil defense does. I'm not sure we'll have time to get to city hall. If they capture us, I'll fix a salad for the Russian soldiers and mix some willow leaves in it.

* * * *

Walking home, Peg watched Joe and Consuela Navarro pull into their carport across the street. The Navarros were older than Peg's parents, but they didn't have any children. In the evenings, Consuela would nod to the neighbors as she weeded around the front bushes. Joe mowed the lawn and talked to ladies pushing strollers or dads walking to the baseball field. Mrs. Navarro's mother lived with them and grew cherry tomatoes in the side yard. Sometimes on the way to the school bus stop, Peg saw the old lady's head at the kitchen window, making sure the children kept their distance. If anybody seemed to even lean in the direction of her plants, she would open the window and shriek at them in Spanish.

On the other end of the street, next door to Phyllis's house, was an even stranger neighbor, a woman who lived alone. She left her house at seven-thirty every morning and came home at five-thirty each afternoon, driving her Dodge Dart all the way into her carport. Nobody else on Arkansas Street parked in their carport. Of course, most carports didn't have room for anything but bikes, dollhouses, and lawn chairs. Or in some cases, large appliances. You could barely fit a Tonka truck on some of the carports, much less a car. But this lady pulled in so she wouldn't have to talk to anybody.

Miss Shirley, Phyllis's mother, once waited in her side yard, pretending to prune the ligustrum, and talked to her for a few minutes. Miss Shirley said she had an evil eye. That's when Phyllis and Peg started thinking she might be a witch. It was true that she didn't look much different from most of the ladies on Arkansas, but her house was very suspicious. Most people had curtains on their windows, but hers had shades, always pulled all the way down to the sill. Also, her backyard had a six-foot-high redwood fence. Except for the Witch's yard, you could see through all the chain-link fences around all the backyards on Arkansas, see who needed to mow, who had their inflated pool up, who had a new barbecue grill. What did she do in that backyard that she didn't want anyone to see? Peg was determined to find out.

On their first day as girl sleuths, while the Witch was at work, Phyllis and Peg climbed the fig tree in Phyllis's yard to peer over the redwood fence. This was disappointing. There were some rose bushes, a row of daisies, and two aluminum lawn chairs. "See?" Phyllis said. "Nothing."

"Oh yeah? Then why does she need two chairs?"

Peg climbed up to a higher branch, which actually stretched over the fence and into the yard. When they saw the Dodge Dart pull into the driveway Phyllis jumped and ran, and Peg grabbed the trunk like a fire pole and slid down. By the time Peg hit the ground, her legs were scraped and bloody.

They went in to clean up in the pleasant air-conditioned coolness of the Browns' house. The only moving air in the Hennessy house was from the giant attic fan in the hall, and that was only about half a degree cooler than outside. When it rained in the afternoon—about every day—they had to turn off the fan or it would draw puddles of water in through the windows.

Peg used toilet paper to wipe all the blood off her legs, but some of it had gotten onto her shorts.

I am still thinking about the Witch as I clear the table after dinner. Phyllis and I need to do some more sleuthing. Then Mama asks me to help with the dishes.

I went over to the sink and turned on the water. "I know you want to go out and play, Peg, but I thought we could talk for a bit."

Play? Does she think I'm six years old?

"Well." Mama handed Peg a plate, which she rinsed and placed on the drain board. Then two forks. Peg put them in the silverware holder. Then a saucer. Peg placed it at the opposite end of the drain board from the plate.

Another plate. A knife. Two spoons.

"Well." Mama stood there, her hands in the dishwater. Peg turned off the faucet. Daddy got mad when the water was left running.

"Can I go now, Mama?"

"Peg, do you remember when Miss Sue had Anthony?"

"Yes."

"Remember how her tummy got big before that?"

"Sure, that was the baby inside. Like when you had Janie."

"Right. Well something happens to ladies so they can have babies."

"But only if they're married. Otherwise, it's a sin, Sister said."

"That's right."

"But Mary wasn't married when she had Jesus."

"Well, that was different, it was Jesus. And it was a long time ago."

"I don't see why it should be a sin now if it wasn't a sin then."

"You'll understand when you're a little older. But what I wanted to talk to you about is what happens to girls so they can be ready to have babies when they're older. And married."

Mama soaped up a plate. Peg turned on the water and adjusted it to warm. Mama handed her the plate and started fishing around in the sudsy water for silverware.

Peg was holding a fork when the back door popped open and Michael rushed inside, dirty and breathless. "Mommy, Mommy, Robbie was riding his bike in the street. And the car came. And he gots blood."

Mama ran out the door. Peg turned off the water, pushed past Michael and followed Mama to where Robbie and his bike were sprawled. Mr. Navarro was standing next to his car, which was stopped in the middle of the street. He was talking very fast, in Spanish, and seemed to be almost crying. But it was hard to toll over Robbie's screams.

Mama knelt next to Robbie and ran her hands, still in the

Playtex Living gloves, over his stomach and arms. Then she slid one arm under his head and pulled a rubber glove off with her teeth. Robbie took a breath and stopped crying. Mama cradled his head.

"Okay, okay, Rob, Mommy's here." She put her other arm under his legs and started to lift him away from the bike. Robbie started screaming again. His right leg, tangled in the bike chain, jutted out sideways.

"Didn't see him, didn't see him," Mr. Navarro wailed. Now there was a crowd of people.

Mama turned to Peg. "Go call Daddy at work. Hurry up."

The big dent on the passenger side door of Mr. Navarro's car was his proof. He didn't hit Robbie; Robbie hit him.

Peg called her father's office, but it rang and rang. He must have left already. Mr. Navarro drove Mama and Robbie to the emergency room at Ochsner Hospital. Peg took Janie and Michael by the hand and went to find Danny and Jimmy.

Three hours later, a cab pulled up to the house and Mama carried Robbie in. Peg had made the boys go to bed. Janie was curled up next to Peg on the sofa, sound asleep. Mama was surprised Daddy wasn't home, and she let Robbie and Peg have some ice cream before she sent them to bed.

When Peg woke up the next morning, Mama was sitting on her bed. Sunlight seeped over the top of the pink flowered café curtains.

"Do you have to go back to the hospital?"

"No, Peg, but I have something to tell you."

"Mama, I know babies come out of the mother's stomach."

"It's not that." Mama looked at Peg's desk piled with books, and the vanity table with the pink skirt that matched the curtains. A tear glistened at the edge of Mama's cheek.

"This is such a pretty room," she said.

"I know, Mama. I love it."

"But you liked living in New Orleans, didn't you?"

"Sure, but I like Kenner too."

"Maybe we'll go back to living in the city, what do you think?"

"Really, Mama? Oh, that would be great. Will we get a house near Memere?"

"I think maybe we'll live with Memere. Wouldn't that be fun?"

"I don't think we'd all fit."

"Sure we would."

Mama got up and looked out of the window.

"See, I thought you and I and the boys and Janie would go stay with Memere and Pepere for awhile and that way we won't be stuck out here all summer without a car while Daddy's at work."

"But what about Daddy? Wouldn't Daddy be closer to his work there?"

"We'll see how this works out. Now you help me pack the suitcases."

* * * *

It's been four years since we moved from Uptown New Orleans to Kenner. It was like going to a foreign place, one I only knew from signs along the Pontchartrain Expressway on the way to Old Beach. Kenner, ten miles. Kenner, five miles. Kenner, next right.

At first I thought it would be fun to have a big backyard and our own swingset. Plus a brick house with neat tile floors instead of creaky, splintery wood. And enough bedrooms that I only have to share with Janie instead of all the kids. Plus a kitchen with long smooth counters with tiny sparkly gold stars. Mama and Daddy can afford it because of the GI Bill because Daddy was in World War II.

But it isn't fun being so far away from everything, even the other kids at St. Joan. East Jerusalem is what they call where we live. Or East Jesus.

In New Orleans, I could walk from our house to the Napoleon Avenue library and read at a table in the old brick building, cool and quiet on a hot day. In Kenner, the library is miles away, farther than the grocery, along highways without sidewalks. So when Mama tells me that we are going back to the city, I know God has answered my prayers.

Memere's house on Magazine Street had a big porch with a swing where Peg could sit and read and watch people walk by. At night, before she fell asleep on the sofa in the front room, she could hear the clack of the electric bus. Sometimes, Memere and she would go on the streetcar to shop on Canal Street. They dressed up and wore gloves and had lunch in the restaurant at D.H. Holmes.

On Saturdays, Peg's father would come sit on the front porch with the children while her mother worked on the tomato bushes in Memere's backyard. On Sunday mornings Peg went with Pepere to seven o'clock Mass so he could stay at home with the children while Mama and Memere went to high Mass at eleven. The seven o'clock Mass was very fast and after it was over, they would get doughnuts at McKenzie's and then stop at Rinse's Bar, which was the actual name on the sign in front of the place Pepere called Chavenelle's.

Mrs. Rinse lived above the bar. Stairs back behind the kitchen led to the apartment upstairs. A closet behind the bar had a small window that slid open. When it was slow, like Sunday mornings, the front room of the bar was usually empty. Mrs. Rinse would stick her head out of the little window and say "Sit down, I'll be right out."

Chavenelle would be sitting in the back, by the pay phone. Chavenelle was bald and always wore a white T-shirt, black pants, and sandals with socks. In the mornings, there was always a cup of coffee on the table next to him. Mrs. Rinse would come out from behind the bar with the coffee pot and fill his cup. She brought his lunch and dinner there, too. Chavenelle always ate right there, sitting on a wooden chair at the table closest to the phone, with the newspaper and his little notebook in front of him. If he wasn't on the phone when Mrs. Rinse brought the plate over, he might look up and notice her.

"That's a fine looking piece of roast beef, Miss Anna May."

"Well, thank you, Mr. Chavenelle. I made sure Roy cut all gristle off. I got plenty more mashed potatoes, if you're hungry." But by that time the phone was usually ringing again and Chavenelle was writing in the notebook, so Mrs. Rinse would go back to her customers. After awhile, she would come over again, pick up his plate and bring it back to the kitchen.

Father McCarthy went to Rinse's, though not on Sunday of course. Pepere said one of the Altar Guild ladies told the priest he ought not to go there because Mrs. Rinse was living in sin. But Father McCarthy told her Jesus always loved sinners and Republicans. Pepere thought that was funny.

I love going to Rinse's because it's cool and dark and smells smoky. Pepere never said so, but I figure it's best not to tell Mama and Memere about it.

Something strange, though. It's only Friday and Daddy came over here after work. This is the third time that happened. But before, he would just talk to Mama on the front porch or they'd take a walk. This time, Mama got dressed up and told Memere they were going out to Liuzza's for seafood.

Memere is sitting in the chair by the fireplace when Daddy drops Mama off. On the sofa, I close my eyes and pretend to be asleep. Mama comes inside and sits in the other chair by the fireplace. She tells Memere she is pregnant. Memere says Mama is stupid to have another baby, number seven. Doesn't she have enough already? "I'm too sick to help you this time," Memere says. Mama says she can do just fine without her. Then Mama stands up and goes back out on the porch, slamming the door. Memere starts crying. I go over and sit on her lap and hug her.

"Your mother was the smartest girl in the class when she graduated from Redemptorist," Memere said. "But they gave the scholarship to Alma Montgomery because her family had the butcher shop and they were always over at the convent with turkeys and hams. So your Mama went to work instead of college. Sister Christopher came up to me at graduation. 'Mrs. Freret,' she told me, 'you must be so proud of Mary Frances receiving honors in English and history and science.'

"'Yes, sister,' I said. 'Too bad she didn't have enough dollar signs behind her name.'"

****

In August we move back to Kenner. But Emmaline and her family are gone, and nobody in the neighborhood knows where they went. Not even Miss Shirley, who seems to know most things. "They just up and left," Miss Shirley says when I ask. "Seems like one day that little girl is running around dirty and barefoot, and the next time I look down there, everything's gone but all the oil stains on the driveway."

I look in the windows of their house and the furniture is still there. So, for awhile, I hope they have just gone on vacation. But I really don't think so. And they still aren't back when school starts, so I guess they have moved again.

Then Hurricane Betsy rolled through New Orleans, breaking windows and blowing roofs off and snapping trees like they were matchsticks. The carport blew off the Hennessy house, leaving beams poking through the side of the house like giant bobby pins after you sleep on them. And St Joan of Arc was closed for three whole weeks. But Kenner was lucky. On the other side of town in Arabi, the water rose eight feet overnight and a lot of people died in their beds.

* * * *

Mama is six months pregnant when she gets a call one night from Touro Hospital. Daddy drives her into the city, and when he comes home he tells us we can stay home from school because Memere died.

As the oldest, Peg got to go with her parents to the funeral home. They went down the hallway to a long room, with plenty of lamps. All the furniture was pushed against the walls. Sofas, chairs, tables. There were lots of ashtrays.

The flower smell is almost too much. Mama and Daddy walk slowly toward the end of the room, where two kneelers are arranged in front of a long gray coffin. The lid is split in half, with only one end up. I can see Memere's nose rise from the white satin ruffle around the inside of the coffin. I stand next to Mama, who is holding Memere's hand. A pink crystal rosary is laced through Memere's fingers. Mama is leaning down to kiss Memere's forehead when the double doors of the parlor swing open and bang against the wall.

Cousin Audrey started talking, loudly, from across the room.

"Oh, Mary Frances, I didn't know how I was going to get here, then Jay called and gave me a ride." Mama didn't tell her to hush. She just hugged her.

Cousin Audrey said she had a scapular to put in the coffin, and rummaged under her blouse to dig it out. All sorts of straps came into view. Daddy rolled his eyes and made the sign of the cross, before he reached for the pack of Camels in his shirt pocket and went out the door.

Peg knelt and asked Jesus to get Memere out of Purgatory— quickly. Memere would never wear that black mantilla with the flowery summer dress. And she wouldn't like the dark red paint, almost black, on her lips. Memere always blotted her lipstick, often just grabbing an envelope that came in the mail. Her dresser was covered with envelopes with lip marks on the ends like half smiles.

Cousin Audrey used to teach junior high, till the kids started to get bigger and older and she retired. Out of the corner of her eye, Peg could see Cousin Audrey heading toward her. Peg kept looking at Memere. She reached over to touch the rosary. Memere's hand felt like an inner tube. When Cousin Audrey reached the coffin, she was out of breath, her large bosoms rustling against the front of her dress. You could see why teenage boys would torment her.

"And here's Mary Margaret. Getting so big. Pull up your socks, darling."

It is the middle of the summer. I am lying on the sofa in the front room on Magazine Street, with the breeze coming in through the screen door. Memere plops down next to me, waving one of her hand fans. She holds out the front of her dress and waves some breeze down, then takes more breeze from the doorway and waves it over to me. I laugh. She talks about Cousin Audrey, who just got her annulment. I asked what that means.

Cousin Audrey was beautiful when she was younger, Memere says. Mama was junior bridesmaid in her wedding, during World War II. The groom, Wilfred, was an Army officer. Memere says he looked like Ronald Colman. I don't know who that is but I think she means he was very handsome.

Right after the wedding, Wilfred had to go to England and he didn't come back till after the war was over, three years later. After all that time, though, he only stayed in the house with Cousin Audrey and her parents for a week before he had to go home to Tennessee. They never saw him again.

Aunt Primrose took Audrey to the priest at Our Lady of Good Counsel to get an annulment. Which she only just got now, almost twenty years later, in an official letter from the Vatican. What it means is that Cousin Audrey can get married again and still be Catholic. Memere told me the annulment would've made Aunt Primrose very happy. But Aunt Primrose is dead now. And Cousin Audrey isn't likely to get any proposals.

"You know why that man left Audrey?" Memere says. I knew this was going to be good. I could always tell when Memere was going to say something that children aren't supposed to know.

"Why, Memere?"

"Wore her underpants to bed, every night."

Later, I ask Mama what that meant, and Mama fusses at Memere for talking about it.

"Six children and she's still a prude," Memere says.

CHAPTER TWO

emmaline

EMMALINE REMOVED THE KOTEX pad from the clasps on the belt, carefully scooping up all the glops of gushing blood. She laid the bloody pad on the bathroom counter while she threaded a thick fresh white one through the holes, tightened the belt and pulled her underpants and shorts over it. Blood had leaked onto the underpants, but she didn't bother to change. Then she stood on the toilet and used a bobby pin to pry off the cover of the exhaust fan mounted in the ceiling, the one that hadn't worked since they'd moved to Arkansas Street.

Glancing over to make sure the toggle switch was off, so she wouldn't get shocked, Emmaline lifted the fan down and reached between the studs for the brown grocery bag she'd stashed there. She placed the bloody pad into the bag and put it back between the studs in the ceiling. Four up there now, another four nights of freedom beyond the two or three days left on her period. She replaced the fan cover and jumped down off the toilet.

Merle didn't like blood, so when Emmaline got her period she had some nights off from him coming into her room. At first he'd ask, with his stupid snaggle-toothed grin, about her red-headed friend. So she'd extend, giving herself a week or ten days every month. Then he told her she had the longest periods he ever heard of, which was when she decided to save the bloody pads. Once he actually pulled her pants down to check. So now she wore used pads as long as she could.

He had been coming to her room since before her periods even started. When Emmaline had tried to tell her Ma about it, Ma said Merle was being a good daddy. But Emmaline knew that wasn't right. For one thing, he wasn't her *daddy*, just the man her Ma had married right before baby Jolene was born.

Emmaline once asked Peg if her father did stuff like that. Peg looked so shocked that Emmaline never brought it up again. She wished she could talk to Bonnie Jean, but Bonnie had run away. Ma was mad about it. She said she only had two daughters now. Emmaline knew Bonnie hadn't gone far.

When Peg came over the next afternoon, Emmaline said maybe it would be okay to play detectives after all. She could tell Peg was excited.

"You want to go down to the Witch's house?" Peg asked.

"No, that's stupid." Emmaline stopped, seeing Peg's hurt look. "I mean, you've already done that. I think we need to do some real detective stuff. Like a missing person."

"Who?" Peg asked.

"My sister." Peg looked at Jolene playing with her dolls. "No, my older sister."

"I didn't know you had an older sister."

"Well I do, and she's sixteen. But she ran away from home before we moved here. I heard Harry tell Ma he saw her at the Winn-Dixie, so I'm going to go find her. Do you want to come?"

"How are you going to get there?"

"Hitchhike," Emmaline said.

"Mama says that's very dangerous," Peg replied. "They could kidnap you."

"Harry does it all the time. I even went with him once. He says it's a lot easier with a girl because people aren't afraid to pick you up. And it's easiest of all with a kid."

They both looked at Jolene. "Okay." Peg said. "But maybe she better get a shirt on."

"Yeah, that's a good idea." Emmaline walked to the back of the house and rummaged in a chest of drawers. She came back with a sundress she pulled over Jolene's shoulders and a pair of flipflops. Emmaline looked down at Jolene sucking her thumb, her blue eyes half hidden by uncombed pale blonde hair.

"Where we going, Emmy?"

"A fun place, and I'll get you a Coke, but only if you're a big girl and you can keep a secret. Can you do that?" Jolene nodded. Emmaline took her hand and the three girls headed out into the hot June afternoon.

Getting the ride was easy. As soon as they turned out of the subdivision, a station wagon pulled up next to them. They got in and the driver took them all the way down Williams Boulevard, lecturing them the whole time about how they shouldn't take rides from strangers. Neither of them said anything. Emmaline, sitting in the front seat with Jolene on her lap, stared out the window. When they got within a few traffic lights of the Winn-Dixie, Emmaline glanced back at Peg and nodded at the door. They probably should have worked this out before getting in, but Peg seemed to understand. So when the car slowed at the light, Emmaline yanked her door open and jumped out, pulling Jolene with her. The car stopped short and Peg jumped out too. They stood between two lanes of stopped traffic.

The driver leaned over the seat and started yelling that they were stupid girls and were going to get killed. Emmaline ran across to the shoulder with Jolene. Peg stopped in the middle of the street with the back door of the car wide open. The traffic light changed and the driver in the car behind blew his horn.

"Run, Peg!" Emmaline shouted.

Peg looked at Emmaline, then back at the driver. "You're a stranger, stupid," Peg yelled while slamming the door. The man hesitated, like he was going to come after them, but the car behind honked again. He reached over, pulled the front door shut, and hit the accelerator.

They slid down the embankment. Jolene wailed but Emmaline was laughing, which set Peg off laughing too. "You're pretty brave once you're out of the car," Emmaline said. "We better get going. He might come back."

They walked for two blocks, then watched the Winn-Dixie parking lot from behind a house until they were sure the coast was clear. Then they crossed the lot to the front of the store.

When they opened the door, cool air greeted them like a present, and for a moment they stood inside the grocery, letting sweat and dust evaporate from their arms and legs.

"I want my Coke," Jolene said.

"You have to be good for a little longer," Emmaline told her.

Emmaline looked at the three checkout lines. The one nearest them was closed. A gray-haired woman was ringing up a customer through the middle one. On the far line, a girl with her hair in a net had her back to them. Emmaline knelt down by Jolene.

"Peg is going to take you to get your Coke, okay?" Emmaline handed a dime to Peg. "Keep her by the machines for a few minutes." Peg took Jolene's hand and they walked toward the back of the store.

Emmaline cut through the closed register aisle and headed down a row of shelves. She took a pack of fig Newtons off a shelf, looked at the price and put it back. She went up two more aisles and found a box of corn flakes she could afford. Then she went to stand in line.

Bonnie Jean looked different. At first, Emmaline couldn't figure out what it was, but when she got closer, she saw the huge belly. Bonnie Jean finished ringing up all the groceries of the person in front of Emmaline, ripped off the register tape and a sheet of Top Value stamps and handed them to the woman. The bag boy hefted the last bag into the cart. "Would you like help out to your car?" he asked. The woman shook her head no as Bonnie's eyes met Emmaline's.

"How did you get here?" Bonnie asked.

"Got a ride," Emmaline replied. "How did you?"

Bonnie picked up the corn flakes and pushed some numbers on the register. Emmaline started to hand her a dollar, but Bonnie shook her head. "I'll give you my discount," she said. She ripped off the receipt, wrote something on it and put it in the register drawer.

"Gee, that's awful nice of you," Emmaline said. "A whole box of corn flakes. You're some great sister."

Bonnie stared at her. Emmaline stared back.

"Curtis, would you go tell Mr. Trupiano it's time for my break?" Bonnie said to the bag boy. She pointed to a bench outside the door. "Go wait there," she told Emmaline. "I'll come out in a minute."

"Sure, I've been waiting since Christmas, what's another minute?" Emmaline glanced toward the back of the store. Jolene and Peg were sitting on the floor by the Coke machine. Emmaline walked outside, and the heat hit her like a furnace. At least the bench was in the shade.

About ten minutes later, Bonnie came out and sat next to Emmaline. She reached into the front pocket of her Winn-Dixie apron for her pack and offered it to Emmaline. Emmaline shook her head no. Bonnie took one cigarette out and put it in her mouth while she struck a match and lit. "I'm sorry I didn't say goodbye. I was pretty upset that night I left."

"I guess so," Emmaline said, looking at Bonnie's stomach.

"Yeah, I'm going to have a baby," Bonnie said. "I guess you're going to run home and tell Ma."

"Ma doesn't know I'm here."

"I saw Harry last week. I thought Ma would come then."

"Ma doesn't want to see you anymore. She says she only has two daughters now."

"Is that so? Well I don't want to see her either. Or that idiot she's married to."

"Does she know you're going to have a baby? Is that why you left?" And somehow, between the time the words formed in her brain and they came out of her mouth, Emmaline knew.

Bonnie and she looked at each other. Then Bonnie leaned over, brushed Emmaline's hair out of her face, and kissed her cheek. Like she used to when Emmaline was little and fell down.

"He's not messing with you, is he?" Bonnie whispered. "Because I'll kill him, I will. I told him if I ever found out he had messed with another girl, I would tell Ma and I would kill him."

Emmaline almost let go. Then she remembered Bonnie's temper. There was no way this would end well, for her or for Bonnie. Or for Ma, though that didn't bother her much. And suppose she did run away like Bonnie. Who would watch out for Jolene?

"No," Emmaline said. "He's not."

"Thank the Lord," Bonnie said, and hugged her. Emmaline hugged her back, and Bonnie started crying.

"Where do you live?" Emmaline asked.

"A bunch of us are renting a house out by the lakefront," Bonnie said, wiping her nose on her apron. "It's good. We take turns cooking and cleaning up. I might go back to school, after the baby, and one of the girls who works nights said she'd help me take care of it."

"That's good," Emmaline said.

"Well, I gotta get back to work. You okay getting home?"

"Oh, yeah, sure."

Bonnie went back to the checkout line. Emmaline picked up the bag with the corn flakes and walked around the parking lot to the back of the store. A truck was at the loading dock. She climbed the steps and went through double doors into the storeroom. A man behind a window looked up at her, but didn't say anything. She walked through another set of double doors to the back of the grocery, right by the Coke machine. Jolene and Peg were still sitting on the floor, with their backs against the wall. Jolene was holding an almost-empty bottle.

"Can I have the rest?" Emmaline asked.

Jolene handed over the bottle. Emmaline drained the last sips and put it into the empties rack on the side of the machine. "You ready?" she asked.

Peg and Jolene stood and started toward the front of the store. But Emmaline opened the double doors to the storeroom. "Let's go out this way, in case that guy came back," she said.

"How was your sister?" Peg asked.

"Oh, that wasn't her. I asked the manager and today's her day off," Emmaline replied.

"So we'll come back tomorrow?"

Emmaline took Jolene's hand. Merle was just a stepdaddy to her and Bonnie, but he was Jolene's real daddy. *Surely he wouldn't do anything to Jolene.*

She thought about how Jolene sat on Merle's lap in her underpants, the two of them watching TV.

"No," Emmaline said. "I'm tired of this game."

CHAPTER THREE

mimi

MIMI'S STOMACH AND HER head hurt, so she missed the sailing lesson on Monday. Her brother Eddie got a solo lesson, which was fine with Mimi, because the sailboat scared her. No matter how steady she held the tiller, how carefully she tacked and trimmed, the boat always leaned too far and tried its best to dump her into the bay.

On Tuesday, Mimi didn't feel like getting out of bed, so her mother and Eddie went over to the club to play tennis without her. Mimi didn't mind that either, because Florence sat in the rocking chair in Mimi's room at the cottage in Bay St. Louis, Mississippi, and told her funny stories about all the people who lived in Florence's neighborhood in the Irish Channel, especially the family who lived in the next building over.

"Tell me about JT," Mimi said.

Florence took a sip of her ice tea and wiped the sweat off her face. "Let me see, what's that JT done now? Hmmm. Did I tell you about the time JT's mama was mad at him because she had to go to school and talk to the principal?"

"No, tell me, tell me."

"Okay, Miss Naomi, she told JT to stay inside while she went to see if she could get him back in school. Miss Naomi knows that boy, so she locked the door from the outside, but that wouldn't hold no JT, no ma'am. He climbed out the window and grabbed onto the rain gutter to slide down to the ground. But the gutter wasn't screwed all the way into the bricks so it swung free with him hanging on it. So there he is, going up and down and yelling his fool head off. Good thing he's such a skinny little thing or he'd have knocked his skull on the ground from three floors up."

"How did he get down?"

"I woke Leroy up to go over there and get him. Leroy wasn't too happy, 'cause he had just got to bed and he was on night shift, but he did it. He sure did fuss at JT, told him next time he was going to let him fall down and break every bone in his body."

"Was JT scared?"

"JT ain't scared of nothing. Be better if he was. No, JT says, 'Mr. Leroy sir, I know you a real busy man and I don't want you to be disturbed no more. So I'm going to let you bring me one of them ropes y'all use at the Napoleon Avenue wharf, the real long ones. That way I can tie it on the doorknob and shimmy all the way down by myself. And you don't need to be waking up no more to get me down.'" Florence laughed. "That boy is something."

Florence fed Mimi lunch like she was a baby, holding a wedge of toast to her mouth with one soft hand and the other caressing her forehead. "Come on, little lamb, you not going to get well till you eat something. Eat a little piece for Florence, so I can tell your mama you all well."

But Mimi wasn't well, and when Lady Pamela Percy got back from swimming at the Andrews house on Wednesday, Florence told her she should call the doctor. Lady Pamela went out the French doors and walked across the Lykes' yard to the third house over. Pretty soon Dr. Mason came back with her, carrying his black satchel. Mimi giggled when she saw him. Then her giggles became coughs, and her head hurt even worse.

"What's so funny?" Dr. Mason asked.

"I never saw a doctor wearing shorts," Mimi said.

Dr. Mason took her temperature and got out his doctor flashlight and looked in her eyes and mouth and ears. Then he got out his listener and lifted up her shirt and put the cold metal disk on her chest. Lady Pamela stood at the door, the smoke curling up from her cigarette till the ceiling fan blew it apart. The unbuttoned blouse Lady Pamela wore over her bathing suit quivered in the breeze.

"Aha," Dr. Mason said.

"What is it?" her mother asked.

"Look at this," Dr. Mason said, holding Mimi's shirt up. Mimi's mother walked over to the bed. Dr. Mason turned around, still holding up Mimi's shirt. "For God's sake, Pam, put that thing out," he said. "If not for yourself, at least for your daughter."

"Berch, you are such a bore." Lady Pamela mashed her cigarette into the ashtray she was carrying and set it on the windowsill. When she leaned over Dr. Mason, Mimi could smell her perfume and see her breasts brush against the doctor's shoulder.

"Measles," Dr. Mason said.

Mimi looked down at her white belly. It was covered with pink polka dots. She didn't remember seeing them when she put her pajamas on.

"It's contagious, isn't it?" Lady Pamela asked.

Dr. Mason laughed. "Unless you've had it already, most assuredly."

And that was that. Summer was over. Mimi's father, who usually didn't get to the bay till Friday night or Saturday morning, drove out on the Thursday before Labor Day weekend to pick up Mimi and Florence and bring them back to Octavia Street. Big Eddie decided not to go back to the bay, which meant Florence could go home to St. Thomas Street at night to stay with her daughter and Leroy could work extra shifts at the wharf.

Even though Hurricane Betsy was still headed toward Florida, the weather forecasters were saying that it might turn. So the longshoremen had a lot of work to do, moving things into warehouses and nailing boards and tying things down. Florence said they had to be ready, just in case. She seemed pretty happy about that.

"Don't you like being here?" Mimi asked. They had been home for three days, and Mimi was feeling better. Her temperature had been normal for a whole day, and if it kept being normal for another day, she'd be well. Florence was giving Mimi a sponge bath in her bed.

Florence pushed Mimi over a little and sat down on the edge of the bed. "Oh, lambie, of course I do," Florence said. "What you think? Don't I love my little sweet pea?" She pulled Mimi forward and wrung out the cloth. Even with the shades down, the room was warm, and the cool water tickled Mimi as it ran down her back. "But if Leroy can make some more money, we going to get us an automobile."

"So you won't ride the bus any more?"

"It's mostly for Leroy. Lot of the time he has to work late and the buses ain't too regular after midnight. And that man has always wanted himself an automobile." Florence laid the washcloth on the side of the white enamel basin and took a big towel off the chair, wrapping it around Mimi and squeezing her as she patted her back dry. Mimi nuzzled into Florence's neck, smelling all the Florence smells of soap and ironing board steam and sheets flapping on the clothesline.

"Can't you bring Jeannette here? Or I could go home with you. I'm well now."

"Your mama and daddy wants you in your own bed at night."

"I wish you were my mother."

Florence stood up and folded the damp towel. "Don't ever say that, honey. Everybody's got to be with they own family."

She walked over to the chest of drawers and got a shirt and shorts and underpants for Mimi. "I tell you what, though," Florence said as she helped Mimi into her clothes. "You must be getting well, 'cause you starting to get sassy again."

When Mimi's father got home, he said they had closed the bottling company tomorrow, just in case. He was the boss there and he got to decide things like that. Mimi was sitting at the kitchen table while Florence fixed dinner.

"You think it's coming here, Mr. Eddie?" Florence asked.

"Nash Roberts on Channel Six says it looks like it. And Nash is usually right."

Florence lifted a pot of boiling rice off the stove and carried it over to the sink. "I hope it's not going to be too bad," she said.

"Tell you what, Florence," Big Eddie said. "You stay home tomorrow and tape your windows or whatever you need to do."

"What about Mimi?"

"Well, I was thinking I might take her to the office with me in the morning, so I can check that everything's all taken care of. Then, maybe if the storm's not here yet and she feels okay, we might go out to lunch. Would that be okay, little girl?"

"Just you and me?"

Big Eddie stood, walked around the kitchen, opened the pantry door, walked out to the hallway and then came back into the kitchen. "I don't see anybody else here," he said.

Mimi laughed.

"Mr. Eddie, you want me to see if Leroy can get over here tomorrow, help you board up the house?'

"That'd be good, Florence. Now you go on home and call me in the morning and tell me what time Leroy can get here."

* * * *

For Mimi, it was strange being at her father's work with nobody else there. No cars in the parking lot, no Miss Dolly at the front desk, no men in white aprons adjusting things as the Coca-Cola bottles rolled under the carousels with syrup and carbonated water and then got the caps mashed down on them. The conveyor belt that usually squeaked and clinked as the bottles moved up the line was empty and quiet. The whole plant was dark, with big metal shutters pulled closed over the windows.

Big Eddie and Mimi walked around the machines, then up the stairs in the back to the office. Mimi rocked on the swivel chair while her father looked through some papers on his desk. Finally, he was finished.

"So what do you feel like?" Father asked.

"I feel like an oyster po-boy."

"That's strange. You look like Mimi."

Mimi rolled her eyes. Big Eddie always made that joke. "With butter and ketchup," she said.

"Well okay then," he said. "I'm going to show you where they make the best po-boys in New Orleans. But it's our secret, okay? I don't want your mother and her friends going over there and ruining the place."

"I won't tell," Mimi said. "And anyway, they never eat po-boys."

Mimi sat in the front seat of the car, just like a grown-up. Father drove up Magazine Street and parked in front of the snowball stand. He opened her car door, took her hand and they walked half a block to the corner, to a building with peeling paint and a door catty corner to the street.

When Mimi's eyes adjusted to the dark inside, she could see some men sitting on stools at the bar with mugs of beer and ashtrays in front of them. There were six tables with kitchen chairs, but nobody was at the tables. A radio on the bar was blasting out the weather report.

The lady behind the bar had blonde hair piled up real high and cat-eye glasses. Her hair had so many curls it must've really hurt to sleep on all those rollers. "So Eddie," she said. "This hurricane going to hit?"

"I'm afraid so, Anna May. Darn thing turned around and looks like it's heading straight here. Had to close up the plant."

"Oh, that's not good. Who's this young lady here?"

"This is my daughter Elizabeth, but everybody calls her Mimi. Mimi, this is Miss Anna May."

"How do you do?" Mimi said.

"Well I'm glad they don't call you Betsy. Y'all sit anywhere; I'll be right over." She looked around for her pad, which she finally located behind a row of bottles, then ducked under the radio cord and came to their table. The cigarette in the corner of her mouth waggled when she asked if they wanted their sandwiches dressed, and what they wanted to drink. It looked like it might shoot out of her mouth or drop on their table, but it didn't, and finally she left to take their order back to the kitchen.

While they ate sandwiches, Big Eddie talked to some of the men on the stools and a bald man on the side of the bar. Finally, he took out his wallet and walked up to the bar to pay. "That was a pretty big po-boy," he said as they were leaving. "Did you save room for a snowball?"

"There's always room for a snowball," Mimi said. "A small one anyway."

Big Eddie bought two, chocolate for him and nectar for Mimi, who held them while he drove home. They sat on the swing in the backyard, slurping the syrup through straws and scooping soft shaved ice into their mouths with little flat wooden spoons. The blazing sun heated the day. It didn't seem possible to Mimi that a great big storm was on the way.

Big Eddie bought the swing last summer. Leroy helped him hang it, climbing their big oak tree to loop the chain over the strongest branch. The wooden swing was so big and heavy that both men together couldn't manage to hold it still to hook the chain. Finally, they set the swing on two garbage cans while they hooked the chain and hoisted it up.

Sometimes, when Mimi was swinging, she would close her eyes and imagine being someone else. A month ago, right before Mimi and her mother and Little Eddie left for Mississippi, they'd had a birthday dinner for Lady Pamela at Commander's Palace. Mimi had saved her allowance and bought her mother a bottle of cologne from the Katz & Besthoff. Mimi's mother had thanked her, opened the bottle, sniffed it and then put it away. About a week later, she came into Mimi's room and sat on the bed.

"Never wear cheap perfume," she said. "The colored, they always wear too much cheap perfume."

Mimi pushed back on the swing and imagined she was the kind of girl who would know to buy Arpège.

"Guess Leroy'll have to climb up again so we can take this thing down," Big Eddie said. "Can't have it blowing off and hitting something."

CHAPTER FOUR

first semester

THE WOODEN THEATER SEATS in the back of the lecture hall creaked as Peg sat down. She pulled up the swing-arm half desk, and placed the Psych 201 textbook, notebook, and pen from her knapsack on it. Leaning down, she fished out a brush and ran it through her hair. Then she tucked the knapsack under the desk. It was freezing cold in the room. She was sitting right under an air-conditioning vent. She began to pack up and move when students started filing in the end of the row and blocked her.

It's September, and for the first time since I arrived here at Lockett Hall, I look around. Every single person in this class, girls and boys, old and young, is wearing blue jeans and T-shirts or work shirts. Hanging out. Except for the girl who sits down next to me. She seems to be wearing a pajama top over a pair of cutoff blue jeans. She slumps down and closes her eyes.

And what about me? Me, the "M. Margaret Hennessy/ Kenner, Louisiana" who smiles out from the "Who's New at LSU" book in her high school cap and gown photo? Does that girl look happy to be finally moving seventy-five miles up Airline Highway and seventy-five light years from the

*downwardly mobile, cookie-cutter subdivision where she
spent her formative years? Does she look pleased with herself
for taking the Greyhound magic carpet to a complete personal
reinvention?*

*Well, I was. Until I looked around Lockett. What was
I thinking? What idiot, what dolt, what complete and
utter imbecile comes to her first day of college—college not
kindergarten—wearing her white dotted poplin high school
graduation dress? That she sewed on her grandmother's Singer
from an oh-so-sophisticated Butterick pattern? Thank God I
sat up here in the back, where I can't be seen. Mostly.*

*I will not live another eighteen years like this. I will not
even live another eighteen hours like this. This is it. This is the
last time I am Peg, Dope Dunce Dimwit. As of this moment,
today, Peg is history. Ancient. Gone. Dust to dust. In fact, Peg
never left Kenner. She tried to, but she is now officially sent
home, along with her poplin dress. In her place, in Baton Rouge
and henceforward, Dear Diary, I give you Maggie. Maggie the
Cat? No, Maggie the Cool. Wasted, Smoking, Slutty Maggie.*

Professor Heinrich Miller walked in and the lecture hall
quieted. He placed some papers at the lectern and then loosened
his tie. He wore a jacket with patches on the elbows. Peg had
never seen anybody wear one of those except on television.
Miller was short, his hair gray, his beard white.

*He looks like the picture of Hemingway on my paperback
copy of The Old Man and the Sea. I've read his CV so I know
he's ancient, well over forty, but he struts across the stage like
he's the quarterback of the Fighting Tigers. Doesn't he know
that the only reason everybody takes Psych 201 is because it's
all about sex? He probably doesn't even know that everybody
calls him Heinie.*

Miller walked out from behind the lectern, hands in his
pockets, and looked around the room. His eyes went left to
right, down and up the rows, as if he was trying to make eye
contact with every single person. Amazingly, there were only a
few coughs and chair creaks. Nobody talked and nobody looked
away. The eye calisthenics stopped abruptly. He focused toward
the top row. Peg slunk down in her seat, but it quickly became
clear she didn't need to bother.

To Heinie, I am invisible. He starts talking about a syllabus and grading and course requirements, but he isn't looking around any more. He is looking straight at the girl next to me. She must sense something because she sort of looks up without moving her head, then tosses her long blonde hair over the back of her seat. Now he is talking about office hours and how his door is always open. So is his zipper, I bet. The tableau ends abruptly and Heinie starts talking to some kids on the front row. "Perv," the blonde girl says, not even bothering to whisper. *A couple of people laugh, but Heinie doesn't seem to hear.*

After class, the students edged to the end of their rows and then down the stairs. Peg didn't move. Neither did the blonde girl. She turned sideways to look at Peg and pulled her legs in. "Hey, sorry, you can squeeze by."

"It's okay," Peg said, fiddling with her knapsack. "I think I'll copy over some of these notes while they're still fresh."

The blonde looked embarrassed. "Um, I can check your back if you like and loan you my sweater if you need, you know . . ."

She thinks my period has come and that's why I am too embarrassed to stand. If only my embarrassment was that easy to fix.

"Oh, it's not anything," Peg said.

The blonde stood up, yawned, stretched, and then scooped up her purse and book. "I saw you taking notes the whole class. Maybe I can borrow them sometime?"

"Sure."

"Great. See you next time. I'm Mimi Percy, by the way. From New Orleans?"

Nooooo AWWWWWyens? Said as a question, as if she weren't sure where she came from. Or wanted to distinguish herself from all the other Mimi Percys around.

"Maggie," Peg said. "Maggie Hennessy."

Mimi smiled, waved, and turned to walk out, in no particular hurry.

Probably to make sure any boy around has time to see her cutoffs squashed into her butt crack, way above the tan line.

And just like that, Peg was Maggie.

* * * *

Mimi from New Orleans isn't nearly as dumb as she tries to seem. For all her Southern girl wide-eyed wonderment, she is pretty efficient at getting her needs taken care of by other people, including professors who always let her take make-up tests without penalty when she oversleeps or boys who agree to take her less-than-cool friends on dates in the hope that one day, like the Tarleton Twins in Gone With the Wind, they will be allowed to sit next to Mimi at the barbecue.

Since Heinie's is her only class before noon, Mimi likes to use it to catch up on her sleep. She got a box of carbon paper that she keeps in her knapsack, handing me a fresh sheet and some loose leaf each Monday, Wednesday, and Friday so I can take her notes simultaneously with mine, saving me the trouble of loaning her my notebook.

"So," Mimi said one Friday as she fell into the chair next to Maggie. "Are you rushing?"

For a split second, I think she means I need to hurry up and get the carbon paper in place before I miss any notes she might need. But I quickly realize she is referring to the center of the LSU social scene, the Greeks. I start to make excuses about why I'm not going through the achingly stupid ritual by which half the girls in my dorm are attempting to gain the ultimate acceptance of sorority membership, but what is there to say? I can't afford it? (Probably true, but that isn't the reason.) I don't want to? (Definitely untrue.) No, the true answer, the one that nobody knows or ever will know, is that I am afraid of being blackballed. Fear of rejection has been the ruling emotion of my life—up until now.

"Not this semester," Maggie said. "I kind of wanted to get settled, figure out about my classes. I might do next year."

Mimi shook her head. "You are so smart. That's what I should have done. I am *so-o-o* tired all the time. Last night was the ice water party, and I didn't get in until curfew. My big sis says sophomore rush is much easier since most of the members already know those girls and they almost never do blackballs. Not that I'm worried about that. I'm a legacy."

"Your mom?"

"Oh yeah, and my grandmother, and two aunts and four cousins. All Tri Pi. My father says all the girls in our family have little Pis imprinted on their Kodachromes."

"Chromosomes."

Mimi laughed. "Yeah, those—so who are you thinking about rushing?"

"Still looking around."

"What was your mom?"

"She didn't go to LSU."

"Oh, so ya'll are Newcomb snobs?" Mimi raised her eyebrows. "Well, why don't you think about Tri Pi? I was telling my big sis about you letting me use your notes and all and she says we need some smart girls to bring up our GPA."

* * * *

I am spending every Tuesday night at the Pi Pi Pi house. By late fall every pledge is pretty much assured of getting in; the one or two odd rushees who didn't belong were weeded out before Halloween. They all are excited about the formal, when they will become full-fledged Tri Pis, like their mothers and grandmothers. Tuesday night is study night, which is enforced by the senior members. You would think every night would be study night, but enforcing Tuesdays is regarded as a very big deal on Sorority Row. More than that, and the Tri Pis might be thought of as eggheads like the Alpha Gammas, the Jewish sorority. Social suicide.

On Tuesdays at Tri Pi, the double parlor filled with members reading, writing, doing math problems. They stretched out across sofas, cuddled into big overstuffed chairs, sprawled on the floor over textbooks. A few who share classes studied together, cross-legged in small circles on the carpet. Clouds of cigarette smoke hovered above the lamps, gently blurring and softening the scene like Vaseline on a camera lens. Tri Pi Heaven.

Seniors glide over to anybody who appeared to be doing anything unstudious. After one warning, a repeat offender would be written up, resulting in a punishment ranging from having to serve and wash dishes during members' dinner to revocation of privileges, including attendance at parties and the formal.

Maggie was Mimi's guest for study night, also her and several other Tri Pis' unofficial tutor. Sorority Row seemed to have virtually the same system intact as Stonewall Jackson Hall, the jock dorm. Jackson Hall maintained a roster of student tutors in every subject, available to force-feed factoids into the pliable cranium of any offensive lineman or point guard who needs to maintain a *C* average to stay on one of the Fighting Tiger teams. The Jackson Hall tutors received university paychecks.

My lucre is social acceptance: only slightly less filthy.

"Did you get a date yet?" Mimi whispered, not looking at me but staring down at the College Math 101 book spread between us.

Everybody at LSU has to take at least one math course and College Math 101 is the easiest available. For Mimi, though, it might as well be advanced calculus. Pi may be in her chromosomes, but it certainly isn't in her brain cells.

"For what?" Maggie whispered back.

"The formal, silly. You have to ask a guy ages in advance 'cause there's usually more than one dance on the same night. Like I know that Chi O is having theirs the same night as ours and I heard the Thetas might too. If you don't ask soon enough all the cute guys get taken."

"I thought you had a boyfriend."

"Well, *yes*." Mimi rolled her eyes and drew out the word *yes* in an exaggerated Southern accent. "Beau Delery's taking me to the SAG formal too. I was talking about you."

"Well, then, no I don't have a date. I'm not a member."

"Don't worry about a thing, Maggie May. You're going as my guest. I already talked to Debbie Lynn about it." Debbie Lynn was Mimi's sorority big sister. "Actually, it was Debbie Lynn's idea. She was very impressed with my psych grade." Mimi laughed, so Maggie did too.

We both know her midterm grade was courtesy of my notes. But the final exam is a bit trickier. The Tri Pi exam library is available to all members, and it contains copies of past exams in most freshman and sophomore subjects at LSU. I refused to let her copy off me during the exam itself, despite the assurances of several senior Tri Pis that Heinie would never catch us and even if he did, wouldn't do anything about it. But even if Heinie were blackmailed to silence by some past psychological misstep into the world of Tri Pi, I still have my grade to think about. So we work out a compromise.

Professor Miller told the class that the exam would consist of two essay questions, of which they will have to answer one. The Tri Pis had exams far enough into the past to establish that there are only three exam models, which Miller seemed to rotate at random.

So I write three essays for Mimi, one from each of the exam models, which she dutifully copies in her handwriting into three separate marble notebooks. It is possible that this won't work— if, for instance, Heinie rotates the six questions, not merely the three tests or, God forbid, throws in a new question—but the consensus seems to be that this is unlikely.

* * * *

On exam day, all students had to leave their belongings at the door. Each person had to show the proctor a blank marble notebook before being handed a test paper. Three proctors were seated at a long table by the entrance. Professor Miller was nowhere in sight. Maggie removed a pen and notebook, hung her knapsack on a hook, and stood in line to get her exam. When she finally reached the table, she handed her notebook to Proctor No. 1, who fanned through it to make sure nothing was written in it, then passed it down the line. Proctor No. 2, seated behind a stack of mimeographed sheets, took the top exam from the stack, placed it inside the front cover of her notebook, and swiveled the notebook to face Maggie.

"Write your name here," he said, pointing to the top line on the first page of the notebook without even looking up.

Then he slid the notebook to Proctor No. 3, who matched her name against the class list and wrote a number on the top of her exam paper.

"ID," he said, and glanced briefly at the student identification card Maggie fished out of her pocket. He glanced at the card and at Maggie, then handed it back to her. "Leave at least one seat between you and the person next to you," he said.

Maggie was already seated when Mimi sauntered in and slowly made her way across the row of seats, smiling her unworried Mimi smile, tossing her shiny blonde flip and whispering sweet Southern "excuse me's" to the bodies attached to the feet she stepped on. There had been some discussion about whether they should sit anywhere near each other, with the consensus that deviation would be suspicious. Mimi didn't glance at Maggie when she sat down two seats over. She frowned as she read through the exam questions, chewing on her pen. Then she started writing.

Once the proctors finished checking in the class, two of them left. Only Proctor No. 1—Brad, the regular graduate assistant in the class—remained. He periodically prowled the aisles, but mostly sat in front on Professor Miller's stool, reading a textbook propped on the lectern.

I am curious about how Mimi is going to manage the switch, so as I write, I glance over at her occasionally. She is scribbling determinedly in the marble notebook. After awhile, I stop worrying about Mimi and concentrate on my own essay.

"Fifteen minutes," Brad said from the podium. A few students gasped and began writing very fast. Maggie finished her concluding paragraph and began reading over her thirteen pages on the relationship of the autonomic nervous system to the endocrine system.

Heinie had set a ten-page minimum, so I should be good. Mimi too. If I remember correctly, her essay on the other of today's choices, three theories of moral development, is twelve pages long. If she can get to it.

A fire alarm sounded. The deafening cacophony echoed around the auditorium, vibrating through eardrums and blaring into brains. Several students started for the door. Brad looked up, apparently unperturbed by the loud insistent buzzing. "Don't leave without turning in your exam books down here," he said.

"But it's a fire!" one girl called out.

"Don't worry," he told her. "The sprinklers will put it out before it reaches the podium, and Professor Miller has tested marble notebook paper for legibility even when wet." There was a sudden stampede to the front to drop off exams as the alarm thundered on. Brad collected the exams, stacked them, and then looked at those remaining in the auditorium. "You think you're the first ones to think of that?" he asked.

He calmly walked to the edge of the stage, reached behind a panel, and flipped the alarm off.

And in that instant, with attention riveted to the side of the podium, I see a flutter in the periphery of my vision, like one of those books that you fan through and a series of still pictures becomes movement, a dog running or a clown dancing or trees blowing in the wind. A shadow, a lifted pajama top, a flash of bra, a disappearing notebook. Three seconds long—if that.

Mimi was hunched over a marble notebook, writing busily. Maggie edged past her, walked down the stairs, handed over her exam.

* * * *

Three days later, Maggie went to check her grade outside the Psych Department office. The grades were posted by student ID number— not name. There was a note next to Maggie's number. "See Professor Miller." No other number had a note next to it.

I have a bad feeling about this.

Maggie headed back to the Student Union, got a large coffee, and took it out to a sofa facing the Parade Ground to think. To calm herself; to start figuring out her options.

Am I about to be kicked out of the university? Or at least given an F in Psych, which is almost as bad because I'll lose my scholarship? And then what? Sewing curtains and having babies?

Calm down. Unless Mimi copped, there's no way Heinie could know. And I am reasonably sure Mimi at least would have told me if he'd said anything to her. She's a complete blabbermouth. She tells me, Debbie Lynn, or her mother everything that happens to her, no matter how stupid or embarrassing.

Still. I go to the bank of pay phones and call her dorm room. On the fifteenth ring, she picks up.

"Have you checked out your psych grade?"

"Have you checked the time? Shit, Maggie. I didn't get in till one-thirty this morning."

"Have you been to the—"

The line goes dead.

In Mimi's world, politeness and coherence don't exist before noon.

Okay, face the music. I walk back across campus into the Quadrangle.

Butterscotch-colored stucco buildings connected by arched porticos surrounded the grass and live oaks dripping Spanish moss. Allen Hall and the other buildings on the Quadrangle had wood floors and high ceilings and murals painted by artists from the Works Progress Administration. That was when LSU was the pride of the Kingfish: Huey P. Long, Louisiana's governor in the 1920s and senator in the 1930s. You could still see the bullet holes in the marble lobby of the State Capitol where Dr. Carl Weiss gunned down the Kingfish.

Maggie had read the fictionalized version of that, *All the King's Men*, which was written by LSU's most famous professor, Robert Penn Warren.

As I walk toward Heinie's office in Allen, I think about the Kingfish and Willie Stark. I know, intellectually, that this Psych summons is probably no big deal, nothing at all, a misunderstanding. But my heart is heavy, as if I am walking through the State Capitol in 1935.

Maggie's sneakers made barely a sound in the hallway. Professor Miller's door was open, but his desk faced the window. Maggie knocked lightly on the frame.

"Professor?"

He turned around and smiled. "Come in. Miss. . .?"

"Hennessy, Maggie Hennessy, Psych 201?" *Now I am sounding like Mimi.* "Psych 201. I went to check my grades and . . ."

"Oh, yes, Miss Hennessy. Sit down." His chair squeaked as he swiveled around. He pointed to a line of folding chairs against the bookcases. Papers and notebooks were piled on every single one of them. He picked up one of the stacks and put it on the next pile over, clearing a place for Maggie. The beautiful wooden bookshelves were brimming over with haphazard paper piles and books on top of folders on top of more books.

Maggie sat. Professor Miller went back to his swivel chair and sat, folding his arms, looking at her.

"Um, I went to check my grade and it said to—"

"See me, yes."

My face feels hot and my head is swimming. My heart is pounding. It is all I can do not to blurt out, I'm guilty, I did it, but please, please, please don't expel me. Good thing I've watched Dragnet enough to know better. I shift my books on my lap. The books tumble to the floor. Heinie leans down to pick up a couple that slid toward him while I pick up the ones nearer to me. My head feels so queer I almost lose my balance.

Professor Miller turned around and fished through some marble notebooks on his desk. Then he pulled one out.

"Your examination paper, Miss Hennessy." He handed it to Maggie, and waited for her to open it. Maggie steadied the books on her lap and opened the marble notebook. The margins were filled in green script. After a minute, she could see a few words and underlined phrases. Insight. Elucidate. Explication. Amazing for an undergraduate. Writing style. She slowly turned the pages. The comments seemed to be positive. Finally, the last page. A Plus.

"Miss Hennessy, I am most impressed. I usually don't look in depth at the 201 course papers. But Brad insisted I look at yours, and he was right. You truly seem to have a grasp of the material beyond what most first-year students have. More importantly, you are able to express and explain it better than some graduate students. Will you be continuing in Psychology next semester?"

"I haven't figured out next term yet."

"Well if you decide to, I suggest you go up to the 300 series. 202 won't do anything for you. I'll be happy to sign off on you jumping ahead. I'd also like to give you some reading material, if you're open to that."

"Oh, yes."

"And invite you to my Thursday evening graduate seminar, not for credit, you understand, but to show you where we are headed and what you can expect if you care to invest your time and thinking in Psychology."

I thank him and take the books he hands me and head for the door. A close call, but lesson learned. Never again will I let myself be put in danger of losing what I've worked for to help somebody who doesn't want to work. Not even if it's a friend. My knees are wobbly. In the Quadrangle, I take a deep breath and smell the sweet olive trees.

CHAPTER FIVE

second semester

THE FIRST WEEK I'M back in Baton Rouge, I go to Heinie's office after dinner. At first, the six graduate students look at me strangely, but Heinie—they call him "Rick"—introduces me and says I'll be auditing. Brad smiles and waves to me. It's not like any class I've ever been in. They argue with the professor and he doesn't seem to mind, even when one of the girls, Amanda, tells him that what he said is asinine.

After the seminar, the students, all except Maggie in their twenties and working on master's degrees or PhD's, headed over to the Union. It was dollar pitcher night and they drank beer and ate popcorn until almost midnight. At one point, when Maggie was returning from the bathroom, she heard the tail end of a conversation.

"Don't worry about her, she's not his type," Amanda said. Maggie asked Brad about it when he was walking her home to Evangeline Hall. Brad said Rick and his wife had split up because of rumors about him and a student. "But I'm not worried about you," he told Maggie. "You're too smart for that.

"Don't get me wrong, he's a great lecturer, a great teacher. I like him," Brad said. "And who knows if any of that stuff is true. You know about the jealousy and the egos around here."

****

It was Maggie's first levee party. Her date was Pete Wardlaw, a friend of Mimi's boyfriend Beau. Pete and Beau were both members of the biggest fraternity on campus, SAG. Officially, that was Sigma Alpha Gamma. Unofficially, it was known as Sleep and Go. As Mimi explained it, that's because there were so many members that they only have room for them to sleep and then they have to leave the frat house.

In my vast experience of one SAG party, Screw and Go is more like it.

Maggie had been hearing all year about levee parties, from the girls in her dorm as well as from the Tri Pis. A levee party consisted of a bonfire on the backside of the Mississippi River levee, far enough downriver so that campus police weren't a problem. There was music, usually from somebody's car radio turned up. Girls were responsible for bringing blankets to spread on the ground and sit on—or lie under. Boys brought Boone's Farm, or a six-pack of beer or two. If your date was a big spender, maybe Cold Duck. And that was it. *Voila*, party.

Mimi told me to dress warmly so I'm wearing an oversized sweater I snitched from my brother Robbie over Christmas break. It is a Scottish looking thing that my aunt gave him. I know he won't miss it. Plus, of course, blue jeans. Also, my new desert boots. Everybody is wearing them now and I couldn't afford them but I bought them anyway with my check from working in the Speech Department office. I figured I had to when Mimi told me Pete was shorter than Beau. I hate being the tallest girl—HATE IT! Desert boots have only the thinnest suede soles so I won't even gain a quarter inch.

Pete picks me up at my dorm. When I come into the lobby to meet him, he smiles and says I look nice. We've talked on the phone a few times so it's not exactly a blind date. He opens the car door for me. Once he is in the car, he reaches behind the seat and pulls out a huge bottle of apple wine. He unscrews the cap and hands it to me. I take a swig. It tastes like apple juice.

They drove for about fifteen minutes along River Road, passing several bonfires before Pete recognized some cars and pulled off the road to park. He came around and opened the door, hoisting a grocery bag full of clanking glass. Maggie took her blanket and Pete put his arm around her shoulders as they climbed the levee.

Our heights match reasonably well as long as I stay downhill of him. Thank you, desert boots.

On the other side, between the levee and the river, the batture stretched for what seemed like the length of a football field. This was because the river was low. When the snow melted from up north, the river flooded this area. During high water, it could reach all the way to the top of the levee. Maggie had never seen it go over the top, but she had seen it come so close they had to open the spillway to divert the water into Lake Pontchartrain. Her father had to investigate when a barge got loose and ran aground, because that could undermine the levee and cause it to give way. Even at low water, the river slapped over the logs and marshy grass on the batture when ships went by.

There were at least thirty blankets circling the SAG fire. Pete waved to some of his friends. Maggie saw Beau and Mimi at the edge of the group, almost into the trees. She nudged Pete, and they headed over.

"Hi, y'all," Mimi called out, then giggled and hiccupped. "What have y'all got to drink? Beau only bought two bottles of Cold Duck and we're out."

"I think you had enough, honey," Beau told her, putting his arm around her waist and snuggling into her neck.

"Oh, don't be such a daddy's boy, Beau," she said, pushing him away. "Give me some of that apple juice, Pete."

Pete handed over the bottle. Maggie saw a look pass between him and Beau as Mimi took a chug-a-lug swig, leaning so far back that she toppled over. Beau grabbed the bottle before much spilled and handed it back to Pete. Then Beau started to climb on top of Mimi, but she was conscious enough to push him away. "Wouldja just..." she mumbled. Then she turned away from him and curled up for a nap.

Beau kind of shrugged. "I guess I'll go check the fire, see if we need any more wood," he said. Pete and Maggie sat on the blanket. Mimi snored.

"I like to watch the river," Maggie said.

"Yeah?"

"Yeah, my daddy works on the river and he used to take me with him when he had to go investigate things."

"What's he do?"

"Corps of Engineers."

Pete nodded.

Everybody knows the Corps. You love them or you hate them. Mostly hate, for flooding upriver to protect New Orleans or allowing the Louisiana wetlands to deteriorate from saltwater intrusion or doing any number of horrible things, maybe even starting the Vietnam War. At least if you believe the newspapers. Daddy hates the newspapers.

"My dad works on the river, too," Pete said. "Union Carbide. He's night safety inspector."

"Is it dangerous?" Maggie asked. The petrochemical plants between Baton Rouge and New Orleans were lit up like small cities on the river, belching great plumes of yellow and orange smoke into the sky.

They always seem scary. Ready to burn uncontrollably. Or explode. Once there was a guy at church whose face and arms were covered in bright pink scar tissue, stretched tight, and one of his eyes was stitched shut. Mama said he had been in an accident at the Norco plant.

"Nah, they have a great safety record at Carbide," Pete said. "Seven hundred eighty-eight days since the last on-the-job injury, and that was a guy fell in the river when he was fixing one of the pipes over the loading dock."

"Did he drown?"

Pete nodded. "Must've hit his head when he went under," he says. "Body washed up in Luling. Three weeks later." Pete took a swig and passed the bottle to Maggie. "They were in the nine hundreds before that. If they get to a thousand days, everybody in the safety department gets a bonus."

"I guess you look forward to that."

"My mom does. Me, I'd rather have my dad at home at night."

Mimi turned over and sat up. She gave an "*urp*" and headed for the bushes. They could hear her retching. Pete nodded to the apple wine bottle, but Maggie shook her head no. After a few minutes, Mimi returned. Except for her messy hair and some bits of grass sticking to her clothes, she looked much better. She rummaged in her purse, took out a small bottle of Listerine, rinsed and spit. She winked at Maggie and went to stand by Beau close to the fire. After a few minutes they came back, picked up their blanket and headed into the woods.

When Maggie turned back to Pete, his lips were about an inch from hers. He kissed her. They fell back on the blanket and kissed hard and Pete climbed on top of Maggie.

Through my jeans and his, I can feel his hardness as he rubs against me and moans. He sucks on my neck and after a few minutes of breathing hard, groans and rolls over on his back. Most of the blankets around us have either disappeared into the woods like Mimi and Beau or are single humps of rhythmic movement. I wait for a bit, then nudge Pete, who seems to be sleeping.

"I need to get back before curfew."

"Oh, sure," Pete said, jumping up. He tossed the empty Boone's Farm bottle into the woods as Maggie gathered up the blanket.

CHAPTER SIX

formal

THURSDAY NIGHT HAD BECOME Maggie's favorite "class." She was thinking about joining the staff of *The Daily Reveille*, and Moo, one of Rick's graduate students, had been giving her pointers about interviewing with the journalism faculty.

Moo's real name was Mary Eileen Westerhaus. Her nickname was because her family owned the Westerhaus Dairy, which supplied all the milk and cream cheese to the entire LSU campus and most of Baton Rouge. Luckily, she was very small and not at all bovine.

Once, after the other grad students had gone, Moo was still grading some papers, and Maggie stayed with her so that they could walk over to the Union together. But Moo's boyfriend came by with his car. They offered to give Maggie a lift, but Rick said he would. It was too late for the Union by then, so Rick took Maggie to the Lamplighter Lounge on Perkins Road and they had a Tom Collins before he drove her back to Evangeline Hall. They sat in his car and talked about psychology and politics and Vietnam until the flashing porch lights signaled curfew.

Talking to Brad and Amanda and Moo—and most of all Rick—is so different from talking to Pete and Mimi and Debbie Lynn, who never read newspapers and don't seem to think anything matters except for on campus. I doubt if they know who is running for the US Senate, but they could probably name the entire Fighting Tiger football team.

Rick says I have "a mind like a steel trap" and real aptitude for a career in psychology. And that I am very mature, unlike most of his undergraduate students. Rick says I seem more like a senior than a freshman and that once I'm not his student any more, he can see himself in a relationship with me. I wonder how it would feel to kiss somebody with a beard.

* * * *

On the morning of the Tri Pi formal, Beau chauffeured Mimi and Maggie from their dorm to the sorority house to dress. Mimi sat next to Beau in the front seat of his two-seat Sunbeam Alpine, and Maggie sat atop the back of the convertible. It was purple, with tan leather upholstery that could pass for gold, underscoring the fact that every fiber of Beauregard Delery's being was an LSU Fighting Tiger—even though Beau, an accounting major who didn't even need a tutor, was second string on the team. When Mimi's father, Big Eddie Percy, was on the LSU team twenty-five years ago, he returned a kickoff ninety-nine yards for a touchdown in the last five minutes of what had been a o-o game against Ole Miss. TV stations in Baton Rouge and New Orleans reshow the video of the "Percy 99" before the Ole Miss game every year.

Beau has some mighty big cleats to fit into. Before he and Pete pick us up for the formal at the Baton Rouge Country Club, I'll have to endure the Tri Pi Pledge Presentation, when each pledge is escorted down the big winding staircase at the sorority house by her father and then becomes a full-fledged Tri Pi. In the Percy family, this is Christmas Eve and Easter Sunday and every birthday Mimi has ever had all bundled up in one. There have been many earnest discussions about what Mrs. Percy is going to wear and whether Cousin Tish, who lives in Shreveport and is eight and a half months pregnant, should be discouraged from attending.

"I can see that girl going into labor, just to steal the spotlight," Mrs. Percy said.

Mimi's hair was wound around the orange juice cans that she used for hair curlers ("the bigger they are, the more body you get.") She blew on the pink nail polish she had applied about five minutes before Beau picked them up. With her regal bearing and Minute Maid tiara, she rode in the convertible like a princess in her carriage, waving at people walking along Lakeshore Drive. Mimi was enjoying every minute of her day, caring not a bit that she looked like one of the extras in *Queen of Outer Space*. Rod Stewart was playing on the radio, and Mimi sang along. She turned, pointing two newly polished fingers at Maggie like drumsticks.

"Wake up Maggie, I think I got something to say to you . . ."

Beau looked annoyed. He said he was not a Rod Stewart fan. When the song was over, he asked Mimi to find another station. Mimi gave him one of the eye rolls Maggie had become so accustomed to.

"Oh, of course, honey," she said, waving her fingers as if any idiot could see why this was impossible. "I'll do it with my kneecaps."

Beau laughed and reached over the stick shift to pinch her knee, then fumbled with the radio knob. The Sunbeam weaved. Without a seatback to steady her, Maggie fell back onto the trunk and, for a moment, teetered precariously over the side of the car. She caught herself before ending up on the pavement, landing on the twenty yards of white tulle that was Mimi's formal gown.

"Be careful, Maggie May," Mimi said without turning around. "I don't think we'll have time to steam it in the shower if it gets wrinkled." Maggie's formal, a pale blue moiré empire that she sewed, piecing together three different patterns to make it original, was squashed under Mimi's. But then Maggie wouldn't be doing the Staircase Walk.

It was still early when they arrived at the Tri Pi House. They took their suitcases and dresses on hangers and were heading upstairs when the housemother stopped them.

"There's a telephone message for you, Mimi," she said.

"Oh God, I hope my parents aren't going to be late," Mimi said, taking the small pink paper printed with three Pis.

Mrs. Paegel looked troubled. "It's from the Infirmary, dear."

"Oh, probably that flu thing I went in for last week," Mimi said. "I'm feeling better now. I'll call them Monday."

"The doctor said to call as soon as you can."

Even Mrs. Paegel isn't immune from the eye roll. "You go ahead, Maggie May," Mimi said. "Debbie Lynn will show you where to get dressed." Mimi dropped her suitcase next to the wall phone in the hallway. "Wait," she called after Maggie, handing over her gown. "Make sure you hang it on the top of the closet door, so it doesn't get wrinkled at the hemline."

Debbie Lynn showed Maggie to her room and after allowing her ten minutes to dress, told her she'd have to leave; members only upstairs from here on out. "Don't worry, Maggie," she said kindly. "Next year, you'll get to stay."

Maggie went down the back staircase and into the hallway that led from the kitchen into the grand foyer. Since there was no seating in the foyer and it was at least an hour before the Staircase Walk was to start, she sat on a kitchen chair near the French doors. She saw the Percy family coming up the front walkway. There were three blonde middle-aged women, the blondest of whom was Mimi's mom, whom everyone called Lady Pamela, and not as a joke. The other two were her aunts. They were wearing tea-length afternoon dresses in pink, blue and yellow, looking like Easter eggs with arms and high heels. Several younger women were in the group; these were the cousins, with Tish waddling up the rear, one arm leaning on a short man whose shirt looked about a size too big for his neck, the other rested on her enormous stomach. Tish wore a gauzy flowered maternity dress that floated up behind her in the breeze and a contented, superior expression. She stopped for a moment, scrunched up her face and clutched her belly, but nobody was watching.

At the end of the group was Mr. Percy, who was the first to notice Maggie. He took the elbow of the pink Easter egg and they came over, hugged and kissed Maggie.

They think I am a good influence on Mimi.

"I am so glad to see you, Maggie dear, you look gorgeous in blue," Mrs. Percy said. "So much more flattering than those white dresses all the Tri Pis have to wear. You can keep Big Eddie company while us girls go on up."

I smile. I don't think she means to point out the abundantly obvious fact that I am an outsider, not privy to the secret pinky twists or whatever else it is that Mimi is in the process of being initiated into. She is like Mimi, so focused on herself that she doesn't realize how she sounds to other people.

"Shoot, honey," Big Eddie said. "I'm going up too, I'm the one who's escorting her down."

Mrs. Percy rolled her eyes and through the pink blusher, pale blue eye shadow and platinum hair, Maggie could see what Mimi would be in twenty-five years. "Not yeeeettttt, ED-wahd," she said in her best Scarlett twang. "It's Trah Pahs only now. We will call you up when it's tahm." The girls head to the stairs. Mr. Percy grabbed another kitchen chair, pulled it up next to Maggie's and took out a pack of Marlboros, which he offered to her.

"No, but go ahead."

He nodded and lit up, leaning his head back against the wall and closing his eyes. When he exhaled Maggie could smell a tiny bit of Southern Comfort through the general cloud of Old Spice surrounding him. It was a nice smell, and for a moment Maggie couldn't think why it made her feel good. Then she realized that Mr. Percy smelled like Rick, and that they were probably about the same age. But Big Eddie seemed much, much older. Even though his hair was brown and Rick's was gray.

It was a bit awkward in the hallway. Maggie had to scrunch her dress under her, and Big Eddie had to move his legs each time a Tri Pi and her mother arrived or a waiter passed between the kitchen and the reception area. "You must be very excited," Maggie said.

Big Eddie laughed. "As long as Lady Pamela and Mimi are happy, that's all—"

The staccato high heels of the blue Easter egg interrupted them. "Edward, you are needed upstairs," she said.

"I'll be right there, Louisa." He took another drag and looked at his watch. "We got forty-five minutes . . ."

"Edward, now."

There was something in her tone that made him drop his fag, grind it in the floor and follow her. Maggie wondered if Tish was having contractions. In any event, it was easier sitting on her own, especially since she remembered to bring her literature text.

Before she had finished a chapter, Mrs. Paegel bustled in and corralled the audience into the foyer. A pianist was playing generic background music, mostly Broadway show tunes.

Maggie stood toward the back and watched as the current Tri Pis trooped down the stairs, two by two, in their formals. Last was Missy Monahan, the sorority president. The music stopped and Missy introduced herself, pausing for applause even before the crowd realized they were supposed to clap. But they did, and Missy nodded and smiled modestly. Missy was on the homecoming court, so she was accustomed to adulation. She announced that "Official Pledge Presentation" of Pi Pi Pi would now begin.

A hush crossed the room as the first of the thirty-one pledges peeked out from the open door at the top of the stairs. The pianist started on "Thank Heaven for Little Girls" and the tableau began with "Myra Gail Arceneaux." When they reached Larissa Joan Smithers, Maggie realized something was wrong. The presentation was obviously alphabetical, but no Mimi. Maggie looked around and saw none of the aunts or cousins. Still, short of Tish giving birth on Mimi's dress, she couldn't imagine what could stop this Date with Destiny.

"Anne Marie Zimmerman," Missy read out. Maggie glanced upstairs and, thank heaven, saw Mimi queued up at the pledge portal. Tish's obstetrical theatrics were nothing more than a brief delay.

"Elizabeth Rose Percy," Missy said, and Mimi stepped out to the landing. The white dress accented her perfect tan and showed every curve on her perfect body without being the tiniest bit vulgar. Rather than teasing and spraying her hair into one of the elaborate up-dos that some other pledges had, Mimi wore it brushed smoothly over her shoulders, shiny golden waves against her back and arms, testament to the power of orange juice cans. But as she walked across the balcony to meet her escort, it wasn't Big Eddie Percy who offered his arm, but Tish's husband Ray. They marched down the stairs, pausing on the landing for the photographer before joining the rest of the members for a group portrait.

Then the champagne bottles popped and the members and families toasted the newest Tri Pis. Maggie headed right over to Mimi.

"What happened? Where is your father?"

Mimi stared. Up close, Maggie could see that her brown eyes

were red around the edges. "I have no idea," she said. "That son of a bitch."

"What happened?" Maggie repeated. "And where is your mother?"

Mimi sighed, took Maggie's hand, and led her through the hallway to the kitchen, then out the back porch, on the way bumming a cigarette from one of the waiters.

"Big Eddie left. He wouldn't take me down the stairs."

"Why on earth not?"

Mimi went over to the swing and sat down, taking a deep drag. Maggie sat next to her and Mimi kicked off the porch floor, sending them aloft.

"He said he was going to kill Beau."

"What?"

"Don't worry, Mother went after him. She told him she'd drive since he was so wasted. She said he'll probably pass out in the car."

"Why does he want to kill Beau?"

Mimi sighed again and rolled her eyes, but her heart wasn't in it. Rather than superior, she looked pathetic. "Because I'm pregnant."

"Oh God."

"Yeah, that's what I said to that stupid eager beaver infirmary doctor. Why'd he have to call right before the formal?"

There was nothing for Maggie to say to this, except to be in awe of Mimi's ability to focus on a tree in the midst of a raging forest fire.

"I went there last week because I was throwing up and all. I thought I had the flu and they could give me a shot or something so I'd be well for today. And now this."

She took a drag. "Anyhow, Father said he wasn't going to go through any charade of escorting his daughter down the stairs in a white dress. So I told him not to be so high and mighty with me when everybody knows Little Eddie wasn't premature at all. I mean, how many six-month pregnancies have you ever heard of where the baby weighs nine pounds and four ounces?"

Maggie laughed, and Mimi did too. "But he wasn't one bit happy when I pointed that out. And the presentation is starting and this is going on in Debbie Lynn's room and Mother is trying to hush him up so everybody doesn't hear. So then he left and Mother had to go after him to make sure he doesn't kill the boy who's destined to be his grandbaby's daddy. But first Mother got Ray to escort me down."

"Does Beau know?"

Mimi laughed again. Maggie was glad she could see the humor in this. "If he did, he'd kill me. I don't think he'd believe it was a virgin birth."

What am I missing here? I feel like I have walked in on the third act of a play without seeing the first two or knowing anything about the plot.

"Honey, Beau and I have never done it. I mean, we 69'd and stuff like that, but never actually did it."

"So, who is it? Who is the father?"

"Maggie May, for somebody who's so smart you are *so-o-o* naïve. Do you think it was those old tests and your essay that got me an A in Psych? Not that the essay wasn't great, and I do appreciate it, and we had to go that route 'cause the graduate assistant was grading the exams. But even with the exam grade, my average wasn't—" She stopped. "It's that perv Heinie. But I didn't dare tell Big Eddie that, so I let him assume it was Beau."

I feel like I have been knocked on the head, hard. The swing is making me dizzy. I see spots and lights and if I wasn't sitting, I think I would fall down. I hear Mimi prattle on as if she is far, far away, talking to me through a giant bottle of Aunt Jemima's syrup. She keeps talking and all I can think of is Rick.

"But don't you worry Maggie May, I'm going to fix everything. Well, everything that can be fixed at this point anyway."

"Are you going to go to Birmingham?"

"My goodness no, we don't believe in abortion. No, tonight Beau and I are going to go all the way." She stopped the swing and tossed the cigarette butt. "Come on, they'll be here soon to pick us up."

After the formal, there is only one more Thursday night class. I don't go. I see Brad at the Union and he says I didn't miss anything, that he was the only one to show up because Amanda was preparing her defense and everybody else had finals. So he and Rick graded papers. I get all A's and go home for the summer.

CHAPTER SEVEN

bride

THERE IS NO SHORTAGE of bridesmaids at Mimi and Beau's wedding. Along with Debbie Lynn and me, there are three other Tri Pis and two of Mimi's high school friends. Tish is matron of honor but she had to promise to leave the baby with a sitter. Mimi was adamant about no crying babies on her big day. I doubt that the irony even crossed her mind.

Debbie Lynn and Maggie were staying at Aunt Louisa's house in Old Metairie. It looked like any other big brick subdivision house until they drove through an automatic gate set into a ligustrum hedge that had to be six feet deep. The street noise faded away. The driveway curled around to the back, where there was a pool and a tennis court. A black man took their suitcases inside and a middle-aged woman came out. Even if Maggie hadn't been told, she'd have known she was Big Eddie's sister. She had his eyes, large and brown and slightly bulging. Only his looked natural, a little puffy, whereas hers were magnified by eye shadow and mascara and seemed kind of stretched out, like the French twist in her hair was yanking her whole face backward.

Aunt Louisa hugged each of them and then took their hands and led them into the house. "Let me show you your rooms, then come on out and we'll have drinks before we go to the rehearsal," she said.

They went into a wide center hall, and as they were turning to head up the stairs, the front door burst open. Mimi yelped, screamed and tackled them.

"Y'all came, I'm *so-o-o* glad to see you. We are going to have *so-o-o* much fun, y'all! Come on, come on, come on, let's go." Mimi was dancing around the hallway. "Let 'em loose, Aunt Louisa. We are going to paint this town bright red." She took both of Maggie's hands and swung her around into a dance. Debbie Lynn and Aunt Louisa laughed.

"Good God, Mimi, I've got to go to the powder room," Debbie Lynn said.

"Well hurry up, we got to get going, I've only got less than twenty-four hours before I'm an old married lady."

"I must say, I've never seen a happier bride," her aunt said. She pointed Debbie Lynn toward a side hallway. Mimi pulled Maggie to the patio. A large ice chest was on a table and she took out two Dixies, popped the tops, and handed one to Maggie. Then she kicked off her sandals and sat on the edge of the pool, dangling her feet. The aqua water glistened, and so did Mimi.

"Oh, Maggie May, I can't wait for you to see my dress. It's a Priscilla of Boston, Alençon lace with seed pearls sewn into the bodice and we had to rush order it special, but it got here yesterday and it is *so-o-o* perfect."

"I can't wait, too. You sure managed to pull a lot together in a short time."

"Lady Pamela can do anything she puts her mind to. There was no stopping her."

I know I shouldn't care. But I have to know. "Did you ever talk to Professor Miller again, I mean after . . . "

Mimi stopped kicking her feet for a moment. She looked Maggie square in the eye and the Southern belle façade slipped away like a Mardi Gras mask. "Have you got any idea how it is to never be pretty enough, never play tennis well enough, never remember to cross your legs the right way at the ankles? All my life, I tried and tried and tried. And then one day, about the middle of high school, all of a sudden I *was*. Boys started calling me. I went to dances and teas. I made Tri Pi. Then, well . . ." Her eyes glistened for a moment, and she seemed about to say something else.

But the mask came up again. She reached her slim tan arm down to the water and splashed Maggie. "Now I'll be the top bride in the Sunday society section. I love weddings, don't you?"

I want to say something, but I don't know what. So many things you think you know, but you really know nothing at all.

CHAPTER EIGHT
harry

HARRY MADERE LIVED AT the elbow of Jefferson Highway, just past the New Orleans city limits, not nearly far enough to be fashionable or safe, but the rent was cheap and that was important when you only worked when the horses were running. He'd been there for almost a year now, moving back down from Bossier City after being away from New Orleans for a long, long time. He hadn't seen his mother or sisters since the night he drove away from Arkansas Street all those years ago. Harry liked to travel light.

Harry was a pari-mutuel clerk at the Fair Grounds. The hours suited him. He started at eleven, an hour before the track opened, leaving him plenty of time in the morning to spend at the stables, talking over feed and times and injuries with the trainers and groomers. Harry loved horses. Always had. At one point, he thought he'd buy a ranch, but with prices what they were you couldn't get a decent-sized one, so he gave up. Still, a horse was the only thing Harry could imagine himself tied down to. He'd messed up before when he let his mind wander to human fillies and the only way out had been to leave town for a while.

Harry had vowed not to let that happen again, though out

of habit he kept himself pretty portable. No phone number, pay the rent in cash, that kind of thing. But that was before he met Lou-Ann Rainey.

Lou-Ann had dark blue eyes with thick lashes and a turned-up nose in the middle of the palest sprinkling of tan freckles across her cheeks. Her curly hair was dark brown, though Harry occasionally noticed some gray. But what Harry loved most about Lou-Ann was her smile. It covered her whole face. Harry could tell her some little thing that happened at the track, or something one of the grooms said, and Lou-Ann's eyes would crinkle and the freckles on her cheeks would curve upward and finally her lips would part over those perfect white teeth and Lou-Ann would sputter and laugh. And Harry would think that maybe it was time to start thinking about settling down.

Lou-Ann worked the overnight shift in the home of Mrs. Harrison Dufour Percy, who was eighty-eight and required nursing care around the clock. When the day nurse arrived at Mrs. Percy's house on Octavia Street, Lou-Ann would walk to the Nashville bus, transfer at Claiborne, and arrive back at the Riverbend Apartments around a quarter to eight, about the time Harry was getting ready to go to the track. Sometimes they'd go over to Rinse's, on Magazine Street off Napoleon, for a drink. Except when Earl, her ex-husband, was there, as he had been for the past two days. But yesterday when Harry got home, Earl's pickup was gone from the Riverbend parking lot. Harry left his drapes open a crack and laid on the bed with the light off all night, watching and waiting. Earl didn't come back. This time, Harry thought. This time.

At seven in the morning, Harry took a shower. He combed his hair and put on a clean shirt and some cologne. He looked at himself in the bathroom mirror. You could see the crack in the leather where his belt used to buckle two notches tighter. He got out a jacket and hung it on the front door knob. He checked his wallet. Two twenties. *Enough,* he guessed. Then he pulled the desk chair up to the crack in the curtains. He sat to the side. Timing was crucial.

About eighteen minutes to eight, the Claiborne bus rounded the curve on Jefferson Highway from the east, its brakes squealing as it stopped half a block from the Riverbend. Harry's heart started beating faster. He kept his eyes on the street. Forty-five seconds later, he could see the brown coat and white stockings down at the end of the sidewalk. She walked slowly, not in any hurry to get home. Just a few seconds more. He'd deliberately left his car at the far end of the parking lot rather than right in front of his apartment like he usually did. That way, he'd be walking toward her, naturally.

The brown coat turned into the parking lot. Harry took a deep breath. He grabbed the jacket and put it on as he opened the door. Without looking up, he turned and locked the door, then started walking toward his car. Out of the corner of his eye, he could see she was halfway across the lot.

"Where are you off to this early?" she called out.

Harry looked up. "Oh, hi. I'm going out for some breakfast." Harry's heart pounded. "Wanna come?"

"You buying? I'm broke till payday."

"Sure, no problem."

"Let me change real quick. I'll only be a minute."

Half an hour later, they were standing at the door of the dining room at the Metairie Holiday Inn, by an easel with a picture of an orange and yellow turkey over a sign that said: *Family Thanksgiving Dinner. Noon to 6 p.m. Thursday. $4.95 a person, children under 12 free.*

A man with a suitcase-sized briefcase was at the register, counting change with one hand while he guided a toothpick through his mouth with the other. The woman behind the register stared into the distance. Then the man finished counting and picked up the giant briefcase and walked out, the toothpick poking out of the corner of his mouth. The woman, who wore a plastic badge that said *Lilith,* snapped the register shut and looked over at Harry and Lou-Ann.

"Be with you in a minute, hon," she said.

"This is great," Lou-Ann said. "Like being on vacation. There was a place we used to go in Pensacola Beach, Captain Holiday's Inn. I don't think it's the same, though."

"I think they named the chain after the movie with Bing Crosby," Harry said. "You ever see it?"

"I don't think so. What's it about?"

"It's a musical."

"I like music. Dancing, too. Dancing, especially. You know the June Taylor Dancers?"

Harry couldn't say he did.

"They were on the Jackie Gleason show. That's what I always wanted to be, a June Taylor dancer. You know when they lie down in a big circle and put their arms together and kick their legs out and then the camera comes down like a kaleidoscope? That's what I wanted to do."

"Never too late," Harry said as he started to follow Lilith to their table.

"Oh, it is for that," Lou-Ann said. "You have to practice every day from when you're seven or eight years old. It's incredible, the amount of practice they do."

"Pure or chicory?" Lilith asked as they sat down.

"Chicory," they both said at once, and then Lou-Ann laughed. "Nobody but Yankees drink that weak old pure stuff," she said. They ordered eggs and bacon and hominy. Lou-Ann shook her head when Harry raised the cream pitcher. "I got used to black when we were first married, Earl and me. We lived in a trailer on his daddy's property, but we ate all our meals with the family. They had this big round table and they'd all sit around it talking real loud, yelling at each other, you know how those Cajun families do, it was hard to get a word in edgewise. And the salt and pepper and cream and butter always were on the other side and by the time they got passed around, well, if you waited for it the coffee would be cold."

Good, Harry thought. *Good to get it out in the open, the Earl business.* "But you weren't from there."

"Houma? My goodness, no. I'm from Mississippi."

"Biloxi or Gulfport?"

Lou-Ann laughed again. That smile broke his heart. "There are other places in Mississippi, you know. I'm from a little town you probably never heard of, up in the Delta. Grenada."

"So how was growing up in Grenada?"

"Oh, nothing special."

"I bet you were homecoming queen. Or queen of the prom."

Lou-Ann blushed and looked down.

"Come on. Prettiest girl at Grenada High School?"

"No, actually, I didn't graduate." Lou-Ann was still looking down at the paper placemat with stars locating Holiday Inns all over the Gulf Coast. "I . . . I had a baby."

Harry didn't have time to hide his surprise before Lou-Ann looked up. "He died," she said.

For a moment, the old saying came to Harry's mind—was it Mencken? Nelson Algren?—about never making love to a woman whose troubles are worse than yours. But just for a moment.

Lilith plunked two plates on the table and a plastic basket of biscuits. "More coffee?" Harry shook his head.

"It was one of those crib deaths," Lou-Ann said. "Earl Junior. He was three months old."

"Um, so you only had the one?"

"Oh, yeah. We only got married 'cause of the baby, and with Earl always being on the road, you know."

Harry nodded, though truly he didn't know.

"That was how we met, he came through Grenada when I was in my senior year. He was so charming, so mature. He's five years older than me, you know."

Harry nodded again.

"Well, you don't want to hear all about me and Earl."

"No, I do."

So she told him about staying with Earl's family in Houma while Earl was off driving the truck. And then Earl's brother got him a job on the rigs, which paid a lot more money. Then Earl stopped coming home even on his three weeks off, and her feeling funny being there with the family, and her brother-in-law and sister-in-law and their four kids would be at the house, and there she'd be, them all wondering why Earl wasn't coming home but not saying anything about it. But looking at her like it was all her fault. She'd walk into the living room and they'd all get quiet. So she stayed in the trailer a lot. And then they thought she was stuck up.

Harry was letting his ears stay unfocused, not listening to her words but letting his mind wallow in the sweet melody of her voice, its highs and lows telling him when to nod and smile and when to look concerned. Enjoy this, he told himself. Remember this. He looked at her, using the end of her toast to push the last of the scrambled eggs onto her fork.

"Do you think that was the wrong thing to do?"

He had no idea what she was talking about. "That all depends," he said.

"I guess so. In some cases you might say people should try harder to stay together. But how could I try if Earl was never even home? And I was about going crazy in that stupid trailer."

"Yeah, that must've been hard."

"Well, after I filed for the legal separation, the Raineys were mad at me. But what was I supposed to do? I was going to go back to Grenada, but his Mama told me to stay in the trailer and she'd get his daddy to talk to Earl, 'cause you know we were still married until a year after the legal separation. So I started going to night school and I got my GED. I don't know if his daddy ever talked to him but Earl came home one time and told me he thought I had done the right thing. So we got divorced and I came to New Orleans to get my nursing certificate, figuring I'd go back to Grenada after I got it. But this good job came up at Mercy Hospital and I moved in with another nurse and . . . well, I stayed here."

"Funny that you kept in touch with Earl."

"Yeah, I guess it is, given how short a time we were married and all. You wouldn't think so, but he was broke up over Earl Junior. Calls me every year on his birthday. June fifteenth. He'd be eighteen now."

"Well, I guess we better get going." Harry waved to Lilith, who brought over the check.

"This was real nice," Lou-Ann said. "I can talk to you."

Harry dropped her off and headed over to the track. He didn't call her the next day or the day after that. On the third day, after the track closed, he went out for a drink with Louie Quintana, otherwise known as Louie the Stooper.

Louie had been a regular at the track for as long as anybody could remember. He never bet much himself but he was always trying to get a hot tip from the jockeys or the trainers. And he was always looking down, looking for discarded tickets that might be winners. That was why they called him the Stooper. You couldn't get it through Louie's head that nobody's going to toss a real winner. Not even the high rollers. Louie pointed out that a couple of two-dollar tickets would buy you a couple of drinks. You couldn't argue with that. And Louie didn't have anything else to do, having been divorced by wife No. 4 last year and not yet having met his fifth.

"You got to get her off the husband," Stooper was telling him. "Yeah, yeah, I know they like that sensitive stuff, listening to them and all that. But take it from me, it's a fine line. You let 'em go on too much about old Bill or old Howard and first thing you know, she's thinking he wasn't so bad, maybe I should give him another chance."

Harry took a sip of Dixie. The Stooper was warming to his topic.

"Mary Frances Hennessy, she was a one. Fine woman. Very fine woman. Had half a dozen kids, but you wouldn't know it from her body. Not that it was perfect, all athletic and such. No, she was soft, round. Nice breasts, little bit of a belly but nothing to complain about. Very nice thighs. Had been married to a real jerk. Son of a bitch would cat around, then get to feeling guilty and beat her up. You know the kind. But she was Catholic. Even the idea of divorce hit her real hard. Then the guy ups and walks out, moves in with his twenty-two-year-old secretary, doesn't see the family."

"How'd you meet a fine upstanding woman like that, Stooper?"

Stooper looked wounded. "You misjudge me. I don't spend all my time with the likes of you, you know. Actually, Mary Frances lived behind my mama's house. Liked to tend to her tomatoes and such in these tight little shorts. As I said, very nice thighs." He waved to the bartender to refill his Southern Comfort, and took a gulp of it.

"So here it is, year and a half after the guy's doing his secretary nightly, never giving his family the time of day. I'm out pruning Mama's rose bushes," he took another sip and winked at Harry, "and I look over the fence at her putting stakes in these tomatoes, and we get to talking about whether Creoles are the best, and I point out that there is a school of thought favoring Beefsteak, and this goes on for a bit and then I ask her would she like to go down to Costanza's maybe for a po-boy and a beer and she says yes, that would be nice, so there we are the next evening."

Harry waved for another Dixie and a whiskey for Stooper.

"So we're having a very nice supper, she's had a couple of beers. This is a woman who's ripe, if you know what I mean. She's feeling the lack of something but because she's Catholic and all she doesn't even quite know what it is. Maybe it wasn't so great with the old man, but at least it was there now and then, plus you know women are much more sensual once they hit middle age. Contrary to what you hear. My theory is something to do with the impending change. Like they say those kids in South America chew nails 'cause they don't have enough iron in their diet. Body instinctively goes for what it needs. Woman who's forty needs a man.

"Anyhow, as I was saying, Mary Frances is ripe. She's had a couple of beers, feeling good. Face kind of flushed, it's a hot night. She's wearing this sleeveless blouse with the tucks in front, top button open. Little drops of sweat rolling down her blouse. 'You're such a good listener,' she tells me. 'I can talk to you about anything.'

"Now, that was my mistake."

"What, listening?"

"No, not going from that to something about her, you know, like that she makes it easy to be a good listener, she's got such a nice voice, some kind of compliment, turn it on her and on us. Nope, I let her keep going. And of course she gets on the old man and how he used to be so nice to her, back when they were first married, and then he had to work so hard after the kids came and they grew apart, et cetera, et cetera, et cetera. First thing you know this bastard used to give her a blackeye once a week is the Knights of Columbus Husband of the Year."

Stooper shook his head and finished off the Southern Comfort. "Good listener. They say that, and there's two forks in the road. You got to make sure you take the right one. That was my cue with Mary Frances and I missed it. 'Course that was years ago, right after the divorce from Lorraine and I wasn't as experienced as I am now. But let that be a lesson to you, Harry."

Harry emptied the last of the Dixie into the glass. "So what happened after dinner?"

"We walk home, sit on the porch a bit, she lets me give her a peck and goes inside. Next thing I hear, she's back at home with the old man."

CHAPTER NINE

to win

STILL NO SIGN OF the pickup truck at the Riverbend apartments. Harry had seen Lou-Ann around, she had said hi to him real nice and kind of slowed down like she expected him to make the next move, but he didn't. He said hi, nice like, and went on his way. Lou-Ann wasn't the type to say anything, but he could tell she was wondering why he hadn't asked her out again. Harry was taking his time.

On Thanksgiving morning, Harry was headed out to the track early to give himself plenty of time to look at the field. He had a tip on a three-year-old in the seventh, Pardon Me Ma'am, and he wanted to see how he looked after his morning workout. The owner was Sidney Danzer, whose furniture store on Tulane Avenue sold Baroque dinette sets and beds with mirrored headboards. Harry saw Danzer and his wife Raechelle (pronounced Rah-HELL and you cleared your throat between syllables) in their box at the Fair Grounds regularly. Rumor had it that Levitz was giving Danzer's Fine Furniture a run for its money.

Since Danzer couldn't afford to undercut the national chain, he was instead selling his more expensive bedroom "suits" and vinyl sofas on credit to people in the projects. Which keeps the inventory moving but then you have the problem of hiring collectors to go knock on doors for your twenty-five- or fifty-dollar payments on the days the welfare checks arrive. All in all, Sidney Danzer was reported to have had some serious overhead of late, not the least of which was Raechelle, whose house on Audubon Place was definitely not furnished at Danzer's.

So the word was that Sidney was expecting to win big with Pardon Me Ma'am and then sell him to one of the breeders up north around Bossier City. The horse had won a couple of minor stakes as a two-year-old, one of them a claiming race, which is how Sidney Danzer acquired him. But nothing yet this year. His trainer, Mike Hebert, had told Harry in confidence that Thanksgiving would be the day.

Harry mulled all this over as he left the apartment. He had checked his bank account the day before: one hundred forty-nine dollars and change. Not enough to cover the rent that came due next week. So why not go large on Pardon Me Ma'am? He got out the racing form and a pencil and started figuring. If the odds on the tote came down, a win bet wasn't going to pocket him much. But he could wheel Pardon Me Ma'am with the field in the Trifecta and make cute, especially if one of the longshots placed. If he lost, he'd have to clear out, which he might have to anyway. He had nothing to lose. And Harry had a good feeling about Pardon Me Ma'am.

He locked his apartment and headed over to the Chrysler Cordoba, which had seemed sporty-looking when he bought it three years ago, used. Now it was what his stepfather Merle used to call a buckety-buck. Buckety-bucks were about all Harry had ever driven. That could change now. A lot could change. It all depended on Pardon Me Ma'am.

Walking past Lou-Ann's apartment, Harry was surprised to see the door open a crack and to hear her sobbing, the kind that wants to be noticed. He tapped on the door, pushing it open. Lou-Ann was face down on the bed in her nurse's whites, her head buried in the wadded-up bedspread. "Are you okay?" Harry asked, a pretty stupid question considering she obviously wasn't.

Lou-Ann lifted her head up from the pillow. Black smudge of mascara surrounded her eyes like a raccoon's. "Hi, how doing?" she said.

"How'm I doing? That's not the point. What happened to you?"

"Oh, I've been stood up again is all. I don't know why I'm even upset about it. It's not like it's the first time. But Earl had promised he would drive me to Grenada for Thanksgiving. I have tonight off so we were going to drive up as soon as I got off this morning and we'd be there in time for dinner and then not have to come back till tomorrow afternoon. Then last night Earl calls up and says he can't make it back, he's got to stay in Pensacola to make a delivery."

Harry guessed that noncommittal was the way to go at this point. "Those things happen," he said.

"Delivery, bull," Lou-Ann spat out. "More like he's delivering to that woman in Panama City." She started crying again.

Harry stood by the door. On the one hand, here was Lou-Ann and she was probably what the Stoop would call ripe. On the other hand, this jealousy thing made it clear she was still dancing to the tune of Earl. And on the third hand, he needed to get to the track and see Pardon Me Ma'am go through his paces.

"Look, I've got an idea. Why don't you come down to the track with me? I've got to work today but I could get you a good seat. Opening day. It'll be fun."

Lou-Ann sniffed and wiped her nose with a crumpled tissue. "Maybe I could win some money."

"Get changed. Put on something nice. Everybody dresses up for opening day."

They got there at nine. The workouts were finishing, and Pardon Me Ma'am was looking good, not the best of the pack, which was fine. Mike had told him they didn't want to show the colt's stuff too much before it counted. Jose Cartenza, who worked with Mike a lot, was going to ride Pardon Me Ma'am. He was from Cuba and probably would be one of the top jockeys around before too long. Harry's good feeling improved by the minute.

Lou-Ann was having fun. The jockey was showing her around the stables like he owned them. Harry was about to break up the little Cuban's show-and-tell when the Danzers and their entourage swept into the stable.

Sidney Danzer slapped his trainer on the shoulder. Raechelle gave Mike a hug and kissed him on the cheek before stepping back, placing kid gloves on sable hips and looking over at Harry, whom Mike introduced.

"It's so nice to meet you, Mr. Madere," Raechelle said, looking him straight in the eye. "What do you think of our little colt?"

"I think he's a winner," Harry said.

"You better believe he's a winner," Sidney Danzer said. "Right, Mikey boy?"

"We'll do our best," Mike said.

"Right, we're taking it slow," Danzer said with an exaggerated wink. "We better get up there if we're going to eat before the start."

"I hope this smell doesn't stick to your clothes," one of the women said as the group headed for the clubhouse.

"That bunch is something else," Mike said as soon as they were out of earshot. "Looks like Mrs. D had the eye on you."

Harry snorted.

"No, you better watch it. She likes to play around. She used to have a thing with Joe Fenster, you know, the trainer? She'd be doin' Joe in his office while her old man was having his gin and tonic, then she'd be back at the box in time for lunch."

"One of those dames that likes to live dangerously, huh," Harry said. "Can't say the type has ever appealed to me."

"Well, watch it. She likes to fuck with the working class, then when she gets tired of them they tend to be out of work."

Lou-Ann and the jockey came back from their walk. "I got to get to the window," Harry announced.

"Bye, Jose," Lou-Ann said. "Good luck." The Cuban kissed her hand.

Harry settled Lou-Ann in the clubhouse and told the waiter to take care of her. He gave her ten dollars to wager. It was illegal for racetrack workers to bet, so his own action was called in to a bookie.

Pardon Me Ma'am had started the day at seven to two but by the third race was down three to two. Damn Danzers bragging. Lou-Ann waved at him when she placed a bet three windows over. Right before the seventh started, Pardon Me Ma'am was at five to two.

The bell went off and Pardon Me Ma'am was near the back of the pack around the first turn. A couple of others overtook him, but Harry wasn't worried. He'd seen Jose race before and he knew the little Cuban liked to hold back and then finish with a flourish. Around the far stretch, Jose leaned down into the horse's mane and put his face close to his ear. Sure enough, it was like gunning the accelerator. Pardon Me Ma'am smoothly gained speed, passing the fifth, fourth, and third horses without even trying. Then Jose leaned down again and the horse's veins bulged and he strained forward to pass the second horse and was half a length out of the lead. He strained more and the Cuban leaned lower and the horse's nose stretched forward and if there had been twenty feet more to the track he would've had it.

Harry's heart sank into his stomach as Jack Givens announced that Jumpin Jiminy had won the seventh. Then Jack came back on and said there was a question and the results weren't certified. Five minutes later, Jumpin Jiminy was out and Pardon Me Ma'am was declared the winner in the seventh.

Later, after they'd balanced up their drawers and handed the cash over, Gus Chappetta from the next window asked Harry if he'd heard what happened in the seventh. Harry allowed as how he hadn't, but whatever it was was fine with him.

"Well," Chappetta said, "suddenly the race is over and nobody can find Jumpin Jiminy's registration papers."

"What? They got to have those things filed before the season starts."

"Yeah, well, it sure looks strange this horse wins and suddenly got no papers. And it's one of Mr. Northcott's."

Harry said goodnight and went to get Lou-Ann, who was feeling pretty good, with her twenty-five-dollar winnings on Pardon Me Ma'am and an afternoon's worth of mint juleps. She chattered all the way down to the clubhouse door about how much fun she'd had and who she'd talked to and all the things about horse racing that she'd learned.

When they stepped outside, a blast of cold air hit them and Lou-Ann shivered. Harry put his arm around her and she leaned into him as they crossed the dark parking lot. He opened the car door for her and she reached over and unlocked his and he got in and closed the door and she slid across the seat into his arms and they kissed good and long and hard.

"I never enjoyed myself so much in my whole life," Lou-Ann said. Harry could feel her warm breath on the tip of his nose.

"Yeah, well I'm sorry I had to leave you alone."

"Your friends took good care of me," she teased. "I wasn't alone much."

"No, I saw that." Harry smiled back at her. He started the car and backed out and she stayed close to him, her hand on his thigh all the way back to the Riverbend.

"You want to come in for a cup of coffee?" he asked her. "It's instant."

"Sure," she said. She sat on his bed while he fiddled with the hotplate and the jar of Folger's on the counter in the bathroom.

"Not much on the china," Harry said as he brought out two cups, one chipped and the other with the racetrack crest on it.

But Lou-Ann was sound asleep. Harry took off her shoes and pulled the spread over her and lay on the other half of the bed thinking about where this road was going.

Lou-Ann was still asleep when Harry left for the track the next morning. Her makeup had rubbed off on the pillowcase, which had enough white in it that her skin looked a little yellow. In five years, her neck would have lost whatever angles it had left, Harry could tell. He got dressed in the bathroom and tiptoed out of the apartment.

At the cafeteria down by the stables, Harry got some coffee and scrambled eggs and since he was feeling pretty flush, two orders of sausage. He put his tray down at a long table where Mike was sitting with some trainers and back office types. Mike nodded to him and then turned back to the conversation.

"The commissioner's going to be down on Monday," one of the bookkeepers was saying. "Mr. Northcott wanted him to come down today and even called the governor, but finally they decided it could wait till Monday since the commissioner's mother had a stroke."

"Does seem pretty fishy," one of the other trainers said. "I mean, don't they check those things before the race starts?"

"You can bet they will today," said the bookkeeper as he shoveled in a piece of French toast.

Harry looked at Mike. "Old man Danzer must be pretty happy, huh? A win's a win."

"He's talking about selling him," Mike said glumly. "It'll have to wait on what comes out of this, I guess. But I'm not worried. Par's the better animal and he'll keep on winning . . . So what's with this Lou-Ann?"

"A friend, that's all. No big deal." Harry drained his coffee cup and stood up. "You doing some workouts this morning or what?"

After the track closed, Harry went to collect on his bet. The bookie operated out of the back room of Rinse's. Harry bought a round of drinks for the regulars at Rinse's. Stooper came by and the two of them decided to go to the Quarter to hear some music. It was almost five in the morning by the time Harry made it back to the Riverbend.

Inside the apartment, he found a note taped to the bathroom mirror: "Can I have a raincheck on the coffee when I get off?"

Harry went to the pay telephone by the Riverbend office, called the track and told them he wouldn't be in for a few days, that his gout had been acting up and the doctor told him to stay off his feet. He listened while the manager made a crack about smoking and drinking and eating hamburgers. That was the good thing about being in such bad shape, people always believed you when you called in sick. He went back to the apartment and emptied his pockets. Close to two grand, even after last night. Enough to travel the road of his choosing. Travel light, he reminded himself. He pulled the chair over to the window and sat. He watched Jefferson Highway until he could see the sun rising over New Orleans.

Then he stripped the bed, piled his dirty clothes on the sheet and tied it all up in a knot. He pulled his old Army duffel bag from under the bed and took it first to the closet, emptying everything into it, and then to the dresser. Still some room left, so he grabbed a couple of towels and threw them in.

Harry picked up the duffel and the knotted sheet and stuffed them both into the trunk of the Cordoba. He backed out of the Riverbend parking lot and turned west on Jefferson Highway as the Claiborne bus rounded the bend.

CHAPTER TEN

rock

THE YOUNG COUPLE SLEPT entwined and entangled across both their train seats. He, on the aisle, leaned his torso over onto her. Her left leg was tossed carelessly over both of his. Her head rested against the window; her face marked by the three dark circles of her sunglasses and her open mouth, sending gentle snores aloft as she slept. Their clothes were cheap and trendy: torn jeans, tight leggings stretched thin over her huge thighs. Such careless love, such easy devotion.

Emmaline turned away from the two—lovers? Married? No rings, but that didn't mean anything—and looked at Franky, seated next to her on the Amtrak Sunset Limited streaking west to Houston, where they would meet Rock for Thanksgiving. "Look, Franky," she pointed out the window at the oil derricks off the coast. "That's one like Daddy works on."

"No, Mommy, those are the itty bitty rigs," Franky said. "Daddy *used* to work on one of them. But now he works on the biggest rig in the whole wide world."

How do you tell a four-year-old that his Daddy works on that big oil rig because it's in a different state, far enough away that they hadn't heard about the time Daddy beat up his boss? And that Daddy's union rep had made the little rig's owner understand that if he in any way gave Daddy a bad or even indifferent reference for that faraway big rig job, the little rig owner's next ten year's profits would go toward attorney's fees? And that this only came to pass after several anxious months, before they knew if the union would stand by him, and if charges would be pressed? And that was the reality of life with Francis Xavier Thibaut. Also known as Rock.

Emmaline had met Rock when she was reporting a story for the Denham Springs *Chronicle* about the True Faith Oil Refinery, where Rock worked at the time. She'd worn her usual miniskirt and high heels to an interview with the owner about the refinery's spotty safety record. After a few of Emmaline's questions, the owner walked out of his office and began climbing the rigging. Not about to let him get away without answering, Emmaline followed, getting halfway up before she realized that several of the refinery workers were congregating below her. While she was trying to decide whether to continue following the capitalist pig or climb down and yell at the sexist pigs, Rock walked over and dispersed the panty-gazing roustabouts. He punched one who was using binoculars. Emmaline thanked him for what was, to her knowledge, the last gentlemanly thing he ever did. A month later, they were living together.

Then came Frank Jr. and varying instances of people not respecting Rock, or smart-mouthing Rock. Mix in Emmaline's new job at the New Orleans *Times-Item*, which had long and unpredictable hours, and it seemed to Emmaline that Rock was angry more often than he wasn't. After that last incident, when the union got the company to suspend rather than terminate, even the union rep had advised Rock to move on. Since there weren't an unlimited number of skilled technicians willing to stay in the States rather than make lots more money in the North Sea or the Middle East, Rock had the new job in Texas by the end of the first week of suspension.

You didn't say all that to a four-year-old. Especially not to one whose Daddy was perfect.

"Do you want to color?" Emmaline asked.

"Sure, I'll draw a picture for Daddy," said Franky, taking his crayons from his overnight bag.

Emmaline pulled down the seatback table and set him up, then leaned back and closed her eyes. She hoped Rock would be in a good mood. They were going to have dinner with her sister's family in Sugar Land, and Bonnie had offered to babysit so they could have a "romantic evening" afterward. Wouldn't that be something?

She slept through New Iberia, Lafayette, Lake Charles, then started awake in Beaumont. Franky was still coloring industriously. "Who's that?" she asked, pointing to the splotch of red and blue with outstretched arms sprouting below its ears.

"Superman," the boy said proudly. Then he pointed to two figures floating behind him. "And me and Daddy."

"Daddy sure will like that picture. Now how about we look around under the seat and make sure we've got everything? We'll be there soon."

Rock was on the platform when the train pulled in, and Franky waved excitedly through the window. At the door of the train, he broke free of Emmaline's hand, jumped over the steps and ran into his father's arms. Rock hugged and twirled him, then threw him up in the air. Franky squealed in delight, but Emmaline, watching them shift with the crowd at the end of the platform, gasped.

"Rock, be careful!"

"Whaddaya think, Franky boy? Should we let this scaredy-cat girl come with us? She doesn't seem to know how boys do things, does she?"

"Leave her here," Franky giggled.

"Nah, we better take her." Rock reached over and pulled her close. "Cause otherwise how am I going to make a Franky sandwich?" With one arm holding Franky and the other pressed into the small of her back, Rock reached over their son and put his lips on Emmaline's. Franky pushed them against both of them as hard as he could, but Rock didn't let go.

"I'm hungry," Franky wailed. "Can I have a dinner with a toy?"

Finally, Rock moved his lips from her mouth to the edge of her jaw, up to her ears. "I missed you, babe," he whispered. "I want you."

She took a gulp of air and the pounding in her heart sent heat through her throat in waves. He kissed her again, hard and quick, then stepped back and stood Franky at his feet. He hoisted both suitcases in one hand and took her hand in his other.

"Hey, what about me?" Franky asked as Rock pulled Emmaline along. Emmaline took Franky's hand and, still dizzy, leaned on Rock as they walked out of the station.

When they got to the restaurant, Franky immediately announced he had to go to the bathroom. By the time Emmaline got back to the table with him, Rock had already ordered a beer and sent it back for being warm. He was looking over the menu and frowning.

"What's all this stuff about chicken tacos and zucchini fajitas? Why can't they have an ordinary burrito?"

The young waitress came back with her pad and hovered nervously. "They put up a new tap and the bartender says it won't be cold for a few minutes," she said.

"Well shit," Rock said. "You got anything cold in a bottle?"

She rattled off a list of brands, and Rock picked one. She looked over at Emmaline. "Margarita," Emmaline said. "And a Coke," nodding at Franky. "We'll be a minute looking at the menu."

"Yes ma'am," the girl said. When she came back with the drinks, they ordered. The waitress assured Rock that the beef burrito could be had without any vegetables. But the hour of good feeling was over. Rock sat sullenly while Emmaline and Franky played tic-tac-toe and helped Benji the Burro find his way through the maze in the kids' menu. Rock's moods were as changeable as the weather in hurricane season. Now, the barometer was falling. Still, Emmaline had seen it shoot up as suddenly and inexplicably. She was hopeful.

Unfortunately, there was a green chili in Rock's burrito. Emmaline spotted the interloper the moment the waitress set their plates down. She busied herself with ketchup for Franky's fries and chicken nuggets, then reached for the salsa. Rock pushed his plate away. "I can't eat this crap."

"Why don't you send it back?"

"It took 'em twenty minutes to get it out the first time. You two'll be done." He shoved his chair back. "I should tell the manager."

"Rock, it's a pepper, for God's sake. Pick it out and eat the thing."

Rock stood, opened his wallet and threw some bills on the table. His eyes bore into her with such venom that it seemed impossible they had kissed an hour ago. "I'll wait for you in the car." He shoved his chair back in, toppling a water glass and knocking a fork onto the floor. The restaurant went quiet as he walked out the door.

Emmaline concentrated on her plate, her face burning, tears in her eyes. The waitress hurried over. "Is something wrong?" she asked.

"He's not feeling well," Emmaline said. "Bad toothache." She fed a bite of chicken nugget into Franky's mouth while he continued to color Benji.

Toothache, Emmaline decided, that was the ticket. From now on, whenever Rock made a scene in a restaurant, she'd tell the waitress he had a toothache. It was the perfect excuse; it explained the behavior, didn't invite more attempts to appease and didn't make her seem disloyal. Best of all, it was short and universally understood. From now on, Rock's tantrums, snits, and perpetual fussiness would be, to the world, a toothache. Emmaline licked the salt off her glass and took a swallow of tequila.

When she and Franky got to the truck, Rock was asleep, leaning back, his arms folded over his chest. She opened the passenger door, helped Franky and then got in herself. Wordlessly, Rock started the pickup.

By the time they got to the motel in Sugar Land, Rock seemed to have forgotten all about the restaurant. But he was hungry, so he went out for a hamburger while Emmaline tucked Franky into one of the two double beds. Once Franky was asleep, she ran hot water in the bathtub and added one of the mini bottles of shampoo to make it bubble. She thought of the times when Rock would come home and climb into the bathtub with her. She pushed in the lock mechanism on the bathroom door before stepping into the tub.

The warm water enveloped her. Positioning a towel on the ledge behind her head, she sunk in up to her neck and closed her eyes.

When she opened them, a door was slamming and suitcases were being tossed about. Rock was back. Emmaline hadn't brought her watch into the bathroom, but the water in the tub was cold. She reached for a towel, pulled the plug, dried off, brushed her teeth, put her nightshirt on, opened the bathroom door.

Rock was under the covers in the second bed, facing the wall. Emmaline picked up the clothes strewn around the room, releasing the smell of smoke and beer. On the other bed, Franky sucked his thumb as he slept. Emmaline climbed in next to him.

* * * *

Emmaline woke to the sound of the Macy's parade on television. Rock was sitting up, propped against the headboard, Franky on his lap. "Finally," he said, smiling. "Sleeping Beauty awakes."

"I'm hungry, Mommy," Franky said.

"Let Mom stay in bed, Franky. I'll go get us some grub."

By the time they finished breakfast, it was time to leave for Thanksgiving dinner. Bonnie Jean lived with her husband, Angus Sinclair, outside of the Loop, in an area of streets named after towns on the Italian Riviera and backing on manmade canals whose giant watery fingers stretched outward from backyard to backyard to storm drain and then twisted back on themselves. Angus and Bonnie Jean's coral brick home was at the end of Cinque Terre Circle, behind an emerald green lawn and surrounded by neatly shapely boxwood and magnolia trees. The cul-de-sac was already crowded with cars, so Rock pulled into the driveway behind a shiny new Lincoln Continental. "I thought this was just us, just family," he said.

"Well, Angus's family too. And Bonnie said there might be a person or two from his office." Angus Sinclair's law partners included an ex-governor of Texas and two former members of the president's cabinet. As he never tired of telling you.

"Jesus Christ."

They got out and started toward the door. The St. Augustine grass, parched in the afternoon sun, crunched under their feet. Halfway up the walk, the wood and beveled glass door opened and Bonnie came out. "Where have you been? We were going to eat at one and the kids are starved." Her warm hug to Emmaline, then Rock, almost made up for the cross tone.

"Who is this big boy? Em, what happened to my nephew Franky? Did this big boy eat him up?" She reached around

Emmaline to tickle Franky, then grabbed him up and kissed him. "Hmm. You smell like Franky. Did you eat my little Frank?"

"No, it's me, it's me, I'm Franky," he giggled.

"I don't know. I'm going to have to ask your cousin Kyle to check you out on the jungle gym in the back. He'll be able to tell because Franky was always the best climber."

"Oh, boy, I'll show you," Franky said over his shoulder as he ran through the house and out the back door. "I'm still the best climber."

"Wait, Franky, till after—" Emmaline began.

"It's okay, I gave them all some chips and dip to hold them off," Bonnie Jean said, putting one arm around Emmaline and the other around Rock. "Come on inside and get something to drink."

They went into the huge den, where a group of men and women stood circled in front of a projection television. A couple seemed to be watching Texas play A&M. But most of them were clustered around Angus, sloshing the contents of wine glasses as big as ceiling fixtures.

"Now this one, it's relatively young, you need to let it breathe," Angus was saying. He closed his eyes as he swirled and put his nose into the glass. "Yes, this is going to be very nice, once it has a little maturity."

"Honey, they're here." The group turned toward Bonnie Jean. "This is my sister, Emma, and her husband, Rock." She pointed at each person in the circle of acolytes. "Bobby, Janice, Phil, Grace, Amelia."

"Hi," Emmaline said.

"How about a little of this zin?" Angus asked. "It's from a very small winery that BJ and I discovered last summer in the Napa Valley."

"Sure," Emmaline said.

"I better go get some more glasses." Bonnie headed through the family room toward the back of the house.

"I'll go with you." Emmaline and Rock followed her into the kitchen.

"Rock, there's an ice chest with beer outside," Bonnie said, waving at the sliding doors that framed an Olympic-sized pool. "I know you'd rather that, right?"

"Thanks," Rock said as he headed out to the patio.

"What's with the 'BJ' stuff?" Emmaline asked as Bonnie reached into a cabinet for two crystal goblets.

"Oh, you know, hon. Bonnie Jean sounds so . . . cornpone. Country hick-ish."

"And let me guess what great legal mind thought up how to fix that," Emmaline said. "Aren't we ever so fortunate that he was open-minded enough to marry into this family of hillbillies."

"Oh, Em, don't go getting on your high horse," Bonnie said. "What difference does it make what the people at Angus's office call me?"

"I hate to see you giving up your identity to make an impression on a bunch of—oh, never mind, I'm being grumpy. How's everything going in the land of the Longhorns?"

"Great, great, Angus got a case settled that'll make this a very nice Christmas. Which will help because Dharma was accepted at Stanford Law School. Angus is so proud."

"And do we have to call her DJ?"

Bonnie smiled. "Dharma would never stand for that. If there's one thing I've taught her, it's never to let a man tell you what to do." Emmaline smiled at her sister.

"You know Ma's worse," Bonnie said.

"Since it's the umpteenth time you've told me, I guess I do."

"She's sorry."

"Yeah, I would be too if I was preparing to meet my maker with all she has on her conscience."

"She could go any time. Then you won't have a chance to— well, to let her know you forgive her." Bonnie sighed. "Jolene went to see her."

"Jolene is a better person than I am."

"Okay, let's talk about something else. Rock still employed?"

"So far." Emmaline sat down at the kitchen counter and blew her nose. "I don't know how much longer I can . . . he's so angry, all the time."

"Well I'm not going to be an I-told-you-so, honey, but . . ."

"But you told me so."

"Em, you do not need this. Get a divorce."

"What about Franky?"

"You and I of all people should know that staying with a

husband is not always the best thing for the kids."

"This is nothing like that was. Rock is a jerk, but not around Franky. Usually. At least not now that he's working here and we only see him once a month."

Emmaline looked out of the kitchen window. In the backyard, Rock was pushing Franky and Kyle on swings, higher and higher, while the boys laughed and shrieked. She spread her fingers on the counter and rubbed her nails. "He told me once he would kill me if I ever tried to leave. That he would never, ever let me take his boy. And I've seen what happens when he drinks."

"Oh my God, Emmaline." Bonnie looked alarmed. "Angus can get you an order of protection. Or he can find somebody to get you one in Louisiana."

"Don't you dare tell Angus about this. Anyway, he only said it once. I'm sure he didn't mean it." Emmaline picked up her glass. "Come on, BJ, let's go have some of that Napa Valley zin."

* * * *

Donna Joubert was out with her girlfriends at Monroe's in Breaux Bridge when she saw Rock Thibaut from across the bar. Donna had known Rock back when people still called him Frank. He dated her older sister in high school, and she'd watch them leave for school dances, Darlene in high heels, hair teased up high, Frank smiling sweetly and joking with her. At Southwest Louisiana College, Frank became Rock, the star linebacker that nobody on the other team's offense could get around. But Rock's draft notice arrived in the spring, after football season but before he had time to get his grades up to passing. By sophomore year, Rock was in the Mekong Delta and Darlene was engaged to Bobby Aucoin.

Donna went over to where Rock was sitting at the bar and pulled him onto the dance floor for the Cajun two-step. Half an hour later, out of breath and sweaty, they got beers from the bar and walked outside. Rock pulled the tailgate down on his Dodge Ram and she hiked herself up. Rock leaned against the truck, looking back at the lighted building. They drank silently awhile till a car door slammed from the back lot and Rock jumped up, startled. "Let's get out of here," he said. They drove over to Bayou Teche and talked in the truck till the windows steamed.

A few weeks later, Donna got out of Rock's truck on Martin Street and walked the block and a half home. She had pocketed her keys and relocked the front door and was headed for the stairs when the living room lamp flipped on. Daddy was sitting on the couch, hunched down so that his face was in darkness. The lampshade made a circle of incandescence on his white T-shirt, stretched tight across his outthrust belly.

"Where the hell you been?'

"At work, Daddy. You know I have to close up on Thursdays."

"Well, hell. They close up that store at nine-thirty. It is now twenty minutes after midnight."

"Kathy and I went out for a—" Before she could finish the sentence, her Daddy was across the room and before she could duck, he hit her in the mouth. She could feel the warm liquid ooze from the tiny vessels on her lower lip that had been torn open by her upper left canine tooth. She hit the floor, blacked out and woke up midsentence to Daddy's beery discourse on how she was a slut like her sister and what's worse with the same no-good son-of-a-bitch. She could barely see Daddy through the rainbow of fireworks coming out of her eyelids, but knew better than to say anything or even cry. She got up, walked up the stairs and went to bed.

* * * *

The next morning, early, Rock picked up Donna and her suitcase on the corner. He drove her to his trailer at Cocodrie till she could figure out what she was going to do.

CHAPTER ELEVEN

ruby

EMMALINE CROSSED THE MISSISSIPPI River Bridge, exited the West Bank Expressway and drove down Whitney to Opelousas Avenue. She pulled up to the red house across from the Navy base in Algiers and parked. It was smaller than she remembered. There was a new brick front that looked out of place among all the raised wood frame shotgun houses. A big Ford Galaxy was pulled under the carport and it fit so tightly she didn't see how Mrs. Fuchs could have parked it. Emmaline remembered having to edge sideways out of the kitchen door to head for John McDougall High when Mrs. Fuchs had parked too far to one side, and that was before there were these brick columns.

She thought about getting out and knocking on the door. But that would only be putting off what she had come across to the West Bank to do. Hard stuff first, that's what her professor at LSU journalism school had preached. Do the difficult interviews, the important ones; you can always fit the others in later, or leave them out. So she started the ignition and headed to General Meyer Avenue.

She parked under an oak tree in front of the Judah Benjamin Asylum and walked to the front window. A woman in a flowered smock looked up.

"I'm here to see Ruby Jessup," she said.

"I'll check," the woman told her. "You can wait over there," pointing to rows of plastic chairs in the adjacent room.

The room was half full, and Emmaline sat by the window, looking out at the sun-dappled lawn. She could see McDougall from here and remembered how scary it was when she'd started there, one of only a handful of white kids at the school. It had worked out, though. She'd had good teachers, who encouraged her writing, and good friends. She had missed her sisters, but for the first time in her life, she'd lived with people who got up and went to work every morning and had dinner at the kitchen table every night. Mr. and Mrs. Fuchs had three grown children, all living out of state. Mrs. Fuchs told her they had volunteered as foster parents because they liked to have young people in the house. When Emmaline left three years later to go to LSU, Mrs. Fuchs knitted a coverlet for her bed in the dorm room.

She heard steps behind her and turned to see an aide pushing a wheelchair to the edge of the waiting area. An old woman in a hospital gown and robe was in the chair, her arms like withered sticks resting on her lap, bony legs showing between gown and socks. Tubes coming out of her nostrils led to a breathing contraption hooked to the back of the chair. Her gray hair was pulled behind her ears into plastic barrettes.

Emmaline stood.

"Oh, it's you," Ruby said.

"Now, Ruby," the aide said.

"I can go," Emmaline said.

"I didn't ask you to come."

"How about a nice walk outside?" the aide asked. "It's so pretty and not even very cold. Going to be a beautiful Christmas if this weather keeps up." The aide turned the wheelchair and motioned Emmaline to follow her down the hall. Double doors opened automatically and a ramp led to a pavement path around the building.

"You can go around this way, and there's some benches," she said, handing the wheelchair over to Emmaline.

Emmaline pushed her mother up the walk. The sun felt warm on her face, and a slight breeze moved the brown leaves on the lawn. Wheelchair squeaks punctuated Ruby's wheezing.

Each successive breath seemed to require more effort to draw air into the throat, down through the collarbone, into the heaving ribcage. Emmaline stopped in front of a bench and sat down facing her mother.

Ruby looked back toward the home. "My daughter Bonnie Jean come all the way from Houston to see me."

"I thought you only had two daughters. Oh, wait, I guess that's Bonnie and Jolene now."

"You always was a smart mouth."

Emmaline sighed. They could go on like this for an hour, like they had after the first time the school district people came to the house. Ruby had accused Emmaline of alerting the authorities. She didn't seem to realize that teachers have to report it when pupils stop coming to class without explanation. In Ruby's world, husbands disappeared in the night, wives and children started looking for new homes and new means of support and it shouldn't be the concern of any school counselor or social worker. The school district visit had prompted a full-scale investigation that ended with Emmaline and Jolene in foster homes.

"Is there anything you want to say to me?" Emmaline asked.

Ruby looked up from her hands, but said nothing.

"Do you want to say you're sorry you weren't a better mother?"

"It was you that made him run away, always accusing him of things. You're the one that broke us up."

Emmaline began shaking. She could feel tears forming. She strangled the sobs until they became massive hiccups, heaving her shoulders and making her shiver. It had been so long ago, she thought she had exorcised all this. But once again, her willpower betrayed her. She took out a Kleenex and blew her nose.

"You girls was always leading him on, walking around in your little shorts and bathing suits," Ruby said.

Emmaline grabbed Ruby's face between her hands and forced it around, leaning in so close she could smell stale smoke each time Ruby exhaled. "Yes, Ma, you're absolutely right," she said. "He left you. He didn't want you any more. You weren't enough of a woman for him. And I'm the one that let him know it."

A single tear crawled through the wrinkled crevices of Ruby's face, hovering on the edge of her chin. She raised a hand and swatted it away. Emmaline picked up her purse and walked to her car.

CHAPTER TWELVE

porky

PORKY BERGERON USED TO say his life began and ended in a three-day period. On Day One, he graduated from West Jefferson High School. On Day Two, he got married to Frenchy Simoneaux's daughter Sandra. On Day Three, he headed out to the rigs. Twenty-eight years later came the resurrection. That was when Frenchy died and Sandra inherited a third of the family business, Frenchy's Bait Shop. Neither Sandra nor her sisters had any interest in bait, fish, or Cocodrie. Porky, however, was intensely interested in finding a way off the rigs, where you actually had to do real labor for sixteen hours a day on your seven days on. So Porky worked out a deal with his wife's family: Until some future date when a deep-pocketed bait shop buyer pirogued down to Cocodrie, Porky would keep the store going and send each sister a check for ten percent of the net proceeds each month.

In the meantime, Porky lived quite well with his official 70 percent—and 100 percent of cash sales. Not being a greedy man, Porky kept enough on the books to stave off any talk of selling the business. And not being a one-woman man—this, to his credit, he'd only discovered since taking over Frenchy's—he augmented Sandra's 10 percent so she could stay in Westwego, near the grandchildren.

Rock brought Donna over to the bait shop to introduce her, since she'd be staying at the trailer while Rock was on the rig. "She's been in an accident," he told Porky to explain the bruises. By the time Rock returned from the rig, Donna was working in Porky's fish-cleaning and packing services.

A few weeks later, a salesman down from New Orleans asked Donna how to prepare his cleaned fish, and she offered to batter and fry them up for him. The next weekend, the salesman was back with a couple of buddies, all wanting Donna's fried fish.

Porky saw the possibilities. He set up picnic tables in the back, where the screen porch was on stilts jutting into the Gulf of Mexico. Soon Frenchy's fish and po-boys and gumbo and seafood platters were so renowned that Porky got a call from the Houma *Post* wanting to send a reporter down to write about it. Porky discouraged that, since the Simoneaux sisters might feel entitled to a share of the restaurant side if they knew about it.

* * * *

Rock would stop at the trailer before he left for the rig and on the way home. In between, there were lots of people around, truck drivers and doctors and salesmen who'd flirt with Donna when she cooked or brought them Dixie beers. She could have encouraged them, but mostly she didn't.

One night, as she got ready to lock up, Rock was sitting on the porch, feet up on the railing, the bulb by the kitchen sink throwing a parallelogram of light on the table behind him. Blue-gray ripples slapped at the pilings under the porch and led all the way out to where the moon met the Gulf of Mexico.

"What're you doing closing up?" he asked Donna as she wiped the tables. "Where's Porky?"

"Off on his monthly conjugal visit."

"Well then, why don't you bring a couple of Dixies and join me?"

The screen door slammed and a minute later opened again. Donna put two sweating brown bottles on the table and sat down next to him. They drank for a while, not saying a word. Donna set her bottle down, undid her ponytail, shook out her damp hair and ran her hands through it before she pulled it up again and tightened the rubberband.

The trailer was on the far side of the bait shop, away from the single streetlight. The shells on the parking lot crunched under their feet. Then the streetlight flickered, and only the moon lit the way to the trailer.

CHAPTER THIRTEEN

city editor

THE CAB—THANK GOD it was air-conditioned—dropped Peg at the corner of St. Peter and Chartres in the French Quarter. That left half a block's walk, all shaded, to get to the French Consulate's cocktail party at the Cabildo, the old colonial museum in the heart of the French Quarter. The Cabildo was one of the oldest buildings in New Orleans, a city of old buildings. It was built in the 1700s by the Spanish and burned down soon afterward, but was rebuilt. When President Jefferson bought the entire Louisiana territory from France in 1803, doubling the size of the United States, the papers were signed at the Cabildo.

The French consul, Didier Levesque, was greeting guests inside the door. He took Peg's hand, then leaned over and kissed her on both cheeks. "You look enchanting," he whispered. She felt the smallest flick of tongue below her earring. Then he turned to the slim brunette next to him. "This is my wife, Anne-Aimee. Mademoiselle Hennessy, the editor of the *Item*."

"City editor," Peg corrected him as she took Madame Levesque's hand.

"I love to read your newspaper," Madame said. "Surely you know my dear friend Ellen Edwards." Peg opened her mouth to agree that the *Item*'s society columnist was indeed the very finest *journaliste,* but Madame was already signaling a waiter. "Please have a glass of champagne," and turned to the person following Peg.

The Cabildo was packed with doctors and lawyers and politicians and television and newspaper people and Uptown nobility. The assembled body heat was too much even for the room's thick stone walls and floor to cool. Men in linen suits wiped their foreheads with white handkerchiefs. Tiny crescents of moisture darkened the bodices of strapless summer frocks. Peg lifted her glass and winked at Ellen Edwards, who smiled and waved her pen from the midst of a group of women lined up to have their names spelled correctly in Ellen's notebook. Ellen wore a white dress with huge black polka dots and a peplum that ruffled out at her waist, a tiny black hat with a veil extending to her eyebrows, and black kid gloves. Peg saw Mimi and Beau Delery across the room, looking about as happy to be at the party as Louis and Marie Antoinette must have been at the Bastille. She turned to put her glass down and almost bumped into her boss.

"Enjoying the party?" *Item* editor Fred Cronin asked. Fred's seersucker suit was impeccable and his gray-blond hair brushed the top of his aviator glasses. "I'm going for refills. Can I get you one?"

Peg had known Fred since she showed up at his office, clutching her clips from *The Daily Reveille* and the Baton Rouge *Advertiser,* a few months after she graduated from LSU. By that point, Peg had buried her daring college persona, Maggie. But she must have retained some of Maggie's nerve since Fred had hired her and everybody said the *Item* never took students right out of school. Make that almost never.

Most of the reporters Peg knew were either old men or old hippies. Unkempt hair. Shirt and tie over baggy pants or blue jeans, one scruffy sport coat kept at the office. But Fred wore pale yellow or pink or pinstriped bespoke shirts (Turnbull & Asser, Jermyn Street, he'd casually let drop after a trip to London) with collar pins and French cuffs, under impeccably tailored suits. His oxfords always shone with understated burnish (the valet at the Racquet Club) and his hair was trimmed to perfection (Melvin at the barbershop near the Pontchartrain Hotel).

Peg started as a reporter, became a bureau chief and within a few years was city editor, running the daily news operations. She knew she hadn't been Fred's first choice. Rumor had it that she was supposed to be a placeholder for the nephew of publisher Lawson Richardson, who was still at Yale when the job suddenly opened after the previous city editor moved to *The Washington Post*.

Fred took her empty glass and turned to his wife Susan, who was holding a glass of ice against her forehead. "I'm not giving this up until I get a replacement," Susan said. So Fred headed off to the bar.

"How does Fred stay so cool?" Peg asked.

"Embalming fluid," Susan said. "Did you meet the elusive Anne-Aimee? I can't believe she finally agreed to come to our colonial outpost. I was beginning to think he didn't have a wife."

Susan put her arm out as Fred returned with two glasses. He took her empty and headed back to the bar. "Of course, that big French lech might as well not have one." Unlike her husband, who seemed to edit his pontifications more carefully than his newspaper, Susan said exactly what she thought.

"That should be an illegal use of Spandex," she remarked as a middle-aged woman waddled by in a tight strapless dress.

Fred signaled to Susan from the bar. "Time to network," she said. "Have fun."

"I will, thanks." Peg checked her watch, put her glass down on a table and headed outside.

Artists were packing up their works from the fence around Jackson Square. Musicians played for groups of tourists along the closed-off block of Chartres between Jackson Square and St. Louis Cathedral. A palm reader between customers, her long black hair flowing over her see-through tunic, sat behind a card table smoking.

Springtime in New Orleans: the very atmosphere had thickness. You could try to walk into it purposefully, but it slowed you, pushed back at your arms and legs and torso, seeped into pores and follicles, condensed on skin and clothing. It limpened starched shirts and iron wills. Peg figured that was why she had agreed to have dinner with a sports reporter, Gabe O'Malley. She was to meet him in Jackson Square.

The Square was crowded but after a few mintues, she saw him. "I thought we'd go over to Tujague's," he said. "That okay?"

"Great."

They walked through the crowd, awkwardly side by side and only brushing arms by accident, the half block to the restaurant. When they stepped inside, the blast of air-conditioning instantly cooled them.

The tables were full, so they stood at the bar.

"Hey, T-Tom, how you doing?" Gabe called to the bartender. Then he turned to Peg. "Let me guess. White wine."

"I work hard at being predictable."

Gabe ordered a Dixie. He lifted the bottle. "Here's to good company."

"I'll drink to that."

"You're the first woman I ever asked out a third time after she said no twice."

"You're the first man at the *Item* I've ever dated."

The maitre d' tapped Gabe on the shoulder. "Got your table, G."

"Hey, we been waiting forty-five minutes," a woman at the bar complained. The bartender shrugged.

At a small table in the back of the restaurant, Gabe pulled out a chair for Peg. "You got to have the brisket with horseradish," he said. "It's the best thing on the menu."

The courses came slowly, but not the drinks. Gabe talked about growing up downtown, cutting class at Holy Cross High School and taking the St. Claude bus to Esplanade to watch the prostitutes promenade up and down the edge of the Quarter. About going to Vietnam and smoking dope and getting shot at and shooting back at people he couldn't see. About coming home and working odd jobs till he earned his degree. And finally, getting paid to do what he'd always wanted to do, write for the sports section of the *Item*. He looked Peg straight in the eye as he talked, and twined his fingers in hers.

When they'd finished, Gabe paid the bill and they walked out onto Decatur Street, which was still packed with people and cars even though it was late. They said their good-nights and Peg declined Gabe's offer of a ride home. She stepped off the curb, raising her arm for a taxi, and her heel caught in a rut in the pavement. A horn blared. Peg tottered. She felt her dress blow up and the side mirror of a passing car brushed her hand. She fell backward on the sidewalk.

"Was she hit?" a woman asked.

"Drunk," her companion muttered.

Peg sat up and looked at her torn pantyhose and bloody knee. Satisfied that there would be no ambulances or corpses, the crowd dispersed. Gabe took her arm and helped her up. "Are you okay?" he asked.

"All but my dignity," Peg said. The heel had broken off one of Peg's shoes and she picked it up, then took off both shoes.

"I think we need some coffee," Gabe said. They slowly crossed Decatur, Peg trying to avoid pebbles on her bare feet, to Café du Monde.

They sat at the edge of the café, near the street, watching the people and traffic. A Vietnamese waiter took their order: two coffees and one order of beignets, the delicious fried doughnuts covered in powdered sugar, to split. From Canal Street, they could hear a siren coming down the street, and then a second. Peg felt her purse vibrate and dug out her pager. The city desk number was blinking on the display.

"I'll have to call in," she told Gabe.

She went to the pay phone near the lavatories, found a dime in her wallet, and dialed the paper. Termite Theriot, the overnight clerk who monitored the police and fire scanners, answered.

"Termite, it's Peg. What's up?"

Termite began listing police codes and directions. He had a speech impediment that made it hard to understand him at the best of times. Over the phone, with all the background noise, it was near impossible. All Peg could make out was "four alarm."

"Calm down, Termite, and tell me what's going on. In English, not codes."

"The Cabildo is on fire!" he shouted.

That got Peg's attention. The Cabildo, and most of the French Quarter, was built before the invention of fire codes.

The sirens were almost deafening now, and Peg could see fire engines descending on Jackson Square. On the other end of the phone line, Termite had lapsed back to the police jargon.

Peg listened for a few seconds but quickly realized there wouldn't be a break in the jabbering anytime soom. "Shut up and listen, Termite!"

"You don't have to be like that."

Peg ignored his pique and told him to find the portable telephone, make sure it was charged and give it to one of the reporters. Peg would stay on the scene and direct the reporters and photographers. She told Termite to call in extra help, even if it meant overtime. She hung up, fished out another dime and called Fred. Only the editor could hold the press run, and he would need to alert the backshop foreman to do that if they were to get the story in the early edition.

When Peg went back to the table, Gabe had already paid for the coffee. They headed back across Decatur.

"I've got a camera in my car," he said. Gabe went to get it and they agreed to meet back at the Square. Meanwhile, Peg broke the heel off her other shoe and put both shoes, now flats with curved soles, back on. Walking crookedly was better than walking barefoot around a fire scene.

Chartres Street had been roped off for a block on both sides of Jackson Square. She flashed her press card and saw Bobby Hartley, an *Item* photographer who lived in the Quarter, already shooting. The fire seemed to be coming from behind the cathedral and well past the fire ropes. Peg wondered if it had anything to do with the consulate party.

Flames were visible through the third floor windows, and black smoke enshrouded the Cabildo, the Cathedral, and the Presbytere on the other side. Peg saw the Channel Four News van pull up, but a policeman wouldn't let them turn on St. Peter. The camera guy hopped out while the driver backed down Chartres. One of their reporters tried to duck under the ropes but a cop stopped him, too. Peg smiled. This fire probably wouldn't even make their late news, and by tomorrow morning, the story would belong to the *Item*.

Bobby was shooting the firefighters lugging huge ropes of hose. A cop saw him and tried to make him move back. Peg hadn't seen any *Item* reporters yet, and time was ticking away. The presses take a minimum of four hours to do a run, and the early edition deadline, which went to most of the state outside of metro New Orleans and Baton Rouge, was ten minutes away. To get a full press run, somebody would have to call in and dictate a story. Quickly. That somebody was Peg. She was an editor now, but she'd been a reporter for years before that. To get the kind of detail she needed, she'd have to get behind the ropes. But the cops seemed to be watching every inch.

"Peg!" Gabe called from the Andrew Jackson statue. He grabbed her hand, pulling her toward the other side of the Square near St. Ann Street. They walked near the crowds gathered at the ropes, up St. Ann to the next block. Then they doubled back down Pirates Alley, till they were next to the building. The firemen hadn't gotten back there yet, so they could get close. From behind a door, they heard faint shouts. Gabe opened it and black smoke billowed out, along with a man carrying a large box and some canvases. They helped him into the alley, Gabe shooting pictures while the man, who said he was a watchman, coughed and staggered with his bundles.

"It was coming down through the attic," he said. "I grabbed these but then I couldn't find the door." He set the canvases, swathed in cloth, against the iron fence but wouldn't let go of the box. Peg knew the box must be important.

"What did you bring out?" she asked.

He hesitated. "I wasn't supposed to be in there after hours," he said. "There's been some losses. But I had left my radio and . . ."

"You're a hero," Peg told him. "Everything else might be destroyed, but you saved what's really important, right?"

Peg reached toward the box. He gently put it down, opened it and took out a round object swathed in sheeting. Gabe's camera clicked while Peg took notes. By the time a fireman came up the alley and told them to get lost, she had enough. She couldn't find anybody from the paper with a portable phone, so she ran as fast as she could in her wobbly shoes back to Café du Monde to call the city desk. Luckily, the regular rewrite guy was there so she didn't have to dictate to Termite.

When she finally got home, smelling like smoke, it was close to four in the morning. Peg plopped on the sofa, intending to rest for a minute before getting into the shower. A thump on the porch awakened her; the morning paper, right on time at seven.

When she opened the heavy bundle, it was all there: Right under the headline, *FIRE AT CABILDO*, was Gabe's shot of a sooty fireman holding the Napoleon death mask across the top half of the front page. Right under that was her byline. When you worked at a newspaper, these were the days you lived for.

She quickly showered and headed in to begin working on follow-up stories for the next day's paper. Editors and reporters drifted in, crowding around the city desk for assignments, then headed back out. A little after nine, Fred leaned out of his office and waved his pipe at Peg. "Great job," he says. "Let's do a news meeting in ten."

When all the *Item* editors were gathered in Fred's office, Peg listed what stories the city desk was planning, passing along what she'd gotten from reporters right before the meeting started. In her year as city editor, Peg had learned how to make sure she had new information to pass along to the higher-ups. Everybody at a newspaper wants to feel like they're on top of the latest news developments, even if they never leave their office.

Two police reporters were working on the main story. Some roofers had been working on a leak earlier in the day and it was beginning to look like wires from a soldering iron accidentally left connected might have lit the attic of the two-hundred-year-old building. Fred remarked that the French consul must be relieved, since the morning story had mentioned last night's party. Though Peg's story had included the obligatory line about no cause of the fire having been determined and the investigation continuing, the implicaton was plain.

Peg would work rewrite on the lead story, taking dictation from those doing the actual reporting, since the cop reporters were great at sourcing stories but not so hot at putting them together. She listed the other stories in progress, including one on the last big fire at the Cabildo, in 1788. Fred nodded, sucking on his pipe. Peg knew he'd have a lot of suggestions for what needed to be in all the stories later in the day, but for now, he seemed satisfied.

As she left Fred's office, she saw Gabe across at the sports desk. Fred had actually said it was a great picture "for a sports guy" and Peg walked over to congratulate him. "You can thank me later," he said.

CHAPTER FOURTEEN

shotgun

"YOU WOULD NOT BELIEVE this guy," Mimi was telling Emmaline when Peg arrived at Arnaud's—late, as usual—after finishing her editing duties at the paper. Peg usually saw her friends separately, but since they both wanted to hear about her date with Gabe, they were all meeting for dinner. Emmaline, the childhood friend Peg had reconnected with when they both were reporters, seemed to have little patience with Mimi, whose life of cocktail parties and Mardi Gras balls was as alien to Emmaline as Emmaline's nomadic childhood was to Mimi. Peg suspected that Mimi sensed Emmaline's disapproval and exaggerated her exploits just to annoy her. Now Mimi was launching into a parody of the French consul. They were already halfway through a bottle of wine and Mimi reached over and filled Peg's glass. Then Mimi took a sip from her own glass.

"Ah, *ma cherie*," Mimi said in her best high school French accent. "Come let me neeble your ear and wheespair to moi about zee sports reportair." As often happened when she'd been drinking, Mimi was her own best audience. She took another sip of wine and then spit it out through her giggles, splashing the tablecloth and the front of her dress. Peg handed her napkin to Mimi, who sopped the stains as she continued talking in mock French, which got less funny to everybody but Mimi the longer she went on. A waiter came over with a new cloth and fresh napkins, and took their orders while the bus boy cleaned the table.

Emmaline was quiet. Peg figured she was annoyed with Mimi and so changed the subject to the Cabildo fire.

"Didn't Termite call you to come in last night?" Peg asked her. "I had you on the list."

"I had to leave work early," Emmaline said. "The babysitter told me if I was late again, she'd quit."

"But I thought Rock was home."

Emmaline stabbed into her pompano and used her knife to shovel a bite onto her fork. "Rock packed up and left yesterday morning," she said. "For good."

"How can you tell?" Peg asked.

"He took his shotgun and it's not duck season. And all his pot," Emmaline replied. "I'm gonna miss the pot." Then she burst out laughing, and Mimi and Peg laughed too. Emmaline seemed to get her spirits back as she told them, yet again, about Rock and the girlfriend in Cocodrie he didn't think Emmaline knew about.

* * * *

After they split the check, Mimi went home and Emmaline took Peg back to the *Item* so she could see how the Cabildo stories were shaping up. Most of the reporters and editors had finished for the day. "There's some police officers looking for Emmaline," the night editor told them. He handed Peg two business cards from the Terrebonne Parish sheriff's office. "I put them in Fred's office."

The officers stood when Peg and Emmaline went into the office. "Mrs. Thibault?" the older, heavier one asked.

"Mackey," Emmaline said. "*Ms.* Mackey."

"Are you the wife of Francis Thibaut?"

Emmaline nodded. The two deputies looked at each other. The older one began talking. As well as the sheriff's office could piece things together, Rock had gotten an anonymous phone call and then loaded his pickup truck, crossed the Huey Long Bridge and headed down Highway 90 through the shacks of Boutte and the sugarcane fields of Des Allemands and the swamps and canals around Raceland and Bayou Blue. They figured it was about six in the morning when he got to Cocodrie. At his trailer, he found Donna in bed. Porky was there, too. Rock blew them both away.

It was mid-morning when the bread delivery man called the sheriff, and early afternoon by the time the deputies located Rock's pickup on the edge of the bayou. He was still holding his shotgun when they told him to get out of the truck, and he didn't put it down. So the deputies had to shoot.

Emmaline sat.

"Are they dead?" Peg asked.

"Yes, ma'am," the younger deputy said. "The coroner said Ms. Joubert died immediately and Mr. Bergeron after about fifteen minutes. He had crawled . . ."

"Well, you've already identified Mr. Thibaut, right?" Peg said. Emmaline was staring out the window at the traffic on the Broad Street overpass. Peg put a hand on her shoulder. "I mean, you don't need Ms. Mackey to go down there, do you? Because if need be, I could identify . . ."

The officers looked at each other. The older one swatted the back of his neck. "Damn mosquitoes," he said. "Ma'am, the suspect, I mean, Mr. Thibaut, he's in Charity Hospital. He was helicoptered from Terrebonne General about an hour ago."

Emmaline gagged and vomited onto Fred's ash gray carpet.

CHAPTER FIFTEEN

thanksgiving

IT WAS ONE OF those heavy November mornings in New Orleans that made a person forget that a week ago she thought summer would never end. Mimi Delery maneuvered the big Volvo station wagon off Octavia Street and around to the side driveway of the house she grew up in. The three-story wood frame with a wraparound porch, Corinthian columns, and leaded glass windows took up most of the lot it was on, and the brick driveway had been laid when cars were much narrower. It was a tight squeeze, pulling the dark blue tank in without scraping its mirrors on the house or the boxwood hedge.

She'd been driving the Volvo for three years, and she hated it. She only had one child, so why did Beau insist on this huge car? Beau said it was better for carpooling. And it was big and safe. Big and safe. Like Beau and their house and their life.

She parked, gathered up the pie boxes from McKenzie's and walked up the back steps. Through the French doors, she could see Florence at the sink, her big round arms jiggling a knife staccato-like through an onion.

Mimi rapped on the window.

"You're here awful early," Florence said, coming to the door and taking the boxes. "Your mama isn't even awake yet."

"I thought you could use some help getting ready." Neatly

arranged on the old green metal table were bowls of chopped vegetables. Piles of celery and onion and scallions were on separate cutting boards, ready to be tossed into the roux in the big cast iron frying pan. "But I guess you don't need me at all."

Florence picked up a colander full of green beans and set it down on the table. "Somebody's got the blues today. Here, help me snap these and tell Florence what's the matter." Florence poured herself a cup of coffee and sat down across the table. The chair cushion hissed under her bulk.

"Oh, nothing. The holidays, I guess. Florence, don't you ever get tired of fixing Thanksgiving dinner for other people's families? Don't you want to be with Leroy and Jeannette and her kids? You could have the day off, if you wanted it."

Florence gave her a disbelieving look, like when Mimi used to say she couldn't go to school because she had a tummy ache. "Leroy's got to go to work today like every day, and we'll have Thanksgiving tonight like always. I guess everybody do what they do, Miss Mimi."

The kettle whistled and Florence braced her hands on the table and pushed herself up. "Time for Miss Inez's tea. You want to bring it to her?" Florence poured the boiling water into the teapot and set it on the tray that had already been laid out with a napkin, milk and sugar and a cup and saucer. She handed the tray to Mimi and then held the door open.

Mimi headed down the long hallway, its wide plank floors buffed to an unpretentious sheen under the threadbare Oriental runner. The wallpaper was the same gray floral pattern that had been there since before Mimi was born. They could never rearrange the family portraits along the wall because the paper had faded around them. Not that anybody ever thought of moving anything. She headed up the stairs, past all the old family Mardi Gras portraits, including one of Lady Pamela when she was a maid on the Court of Proteus.

No portrait of Mimi. Instead of a debut, she'd had Teddy.

She opened the door to her grandmother's room. It was dark except where chinks in the shutters threw sunlight stripes on the needlepoint carpet. The gas heater in the corner was cranked up full and the room had Inez's warm, stale, old-person smell. Inez sat on the edge of the bed, her nightgown pulled over her head, her arms raised in a futile attempt to shimmy free of the shroud of flannel. Two pale breasts dangled limply on her torso, its lower half disappearing ghostlike into the sheets except for a balding thatch of pink and gray.

"Jesus, Grandmother, couldn't you have waited for somebody to help you?" Mimi put the tray down and fished the nightgown over her head. Inez reached up and pulled her glasses out.

"What am I supposed to do, sit here all day till Florence or one of you remembers I've got a goddam broken hip and my nurse has the day off?"

Mimi poured her a cup of tea. "Your hip is pretty much mended, the doctor said. You could probably do without the nurse if you wanted."

"Then what, I suppose Lady Pamela will come and hoist me up when I have to pee?"

"You're right, keep Lou-Ann as long as you want."

"Damn right I will." Inez finished her tea. "Now how about you help me get dressed, dearie." A wool shirtwaist was laid over a chair next to an old Country Day School sweatshirt.

"You're not wearing that thing?"

"If your mother doesn't like it, she can damn well get some heat in this old house. Like to freeze my titties off last night. Now, go in the top drawer there and get me some underpants and then those long johns."

Mimi fetched underclothes from the bureau. Inez held her arms out and Mimi slipped a bra over them. Inez lifted her breasts and dropped them into the cups while Mimi wrestled the hooks in back. Then she squatted on the floor and slid the underpants over her grandmother's feet and up to her knees. Soft folds of skin puddled down on either side of her thighbones. She took her cane in one hand and the bedpost in the other and heaved herself up while Mimi raised the underpants.

Finally Inez was dressed. She leaned unsteadily against Mimi's arm. It was a slow trek to the stairs, where Mimi helped her into the electric stair climber and snapped it shut. "Give me a shove," Inez said, "Florence'll get me off."

Mimi flipped the switch, the electric motor lurched forward and Inez slowly descended. Down the hall, through the open door of her bedroom, Mimi could see Lady Pamela seated at the mahogany vanity table. She was brushing her hair, which perfectly matched her gray silk blouse. Her reflection smiled. "You're here awfully early, darling."

As Mimi walked to her room, she knew Lady Pamela had located six and a half extra pounds on her hips, decided the color of her sweater was unflattering, and noted the scuffed heels of her loafers. Lady Pamela plucked a hair off Mimi's shoulder.

"Did Beau have to go to the office this morning?" she asked as she fastened the clasp of her pearls.

"No, I . . . I wanted to get to McKenzie's before all the Boston cream pies were gone."

But Lady Pamela was already in the closet, looking down at the rows of identical flats and low-heeled pumps arranged by hue, starting with black in the front and going through gray, brown, tan, beige, ivory, and white way in the back. She emerged with a pair of dark gray one-inch heels.

"What do you think?" she asked, as if Mimi or anybody else cared what shoes she wore.

"Do you ever think about getting married again?" Mimi asked her.

"That's not something one thinks a lot about," Lady Pamela said as she studied herself in the three-way mirror. She patted her flat stomach and headed into the hall. "Are you coming?"

"In a minute." Mimi lay back on her mother's bed and closed her eyes. The chenille bedspread, still rumpled, smelled of Arpège.

The scrape of metal against the side of the house roused Mimi. Car doors slammed and footsteps pounded on the front porch and a babble of voices drifted into the house like a swarm of insects. The voices hovered in the front hall before separating, and one, a clear lilt, ascended the stairs.

"It's a little early for naps." Tish swept in, slipping off her coat and molting fur and Gucci onto the bed. She sat at the dresser, dabbing on tomato red lipstick and fluffing her frosted blonde hair. She tipped her head back and touched the soft, slack skin on her neck, then tugged up on her turtleneck collar. "Where's Beau?"

"He and Teddy should be here soon," Mimi said. "I came early."

"Well come on down and meet this nice boy that Jessica's brought home from SMU."

Mimi stood and ran her mother's brush through her hair as Tish blotted her lipstick. They could hear Tish's husband bellowing the same annoying refrain he always did whenever he needed something and Tish was out of earshot.

"Where's my bride?" Ray Barrett called out. Ray was a shrewd litigator and partner at the oldest law firm in New Orleans. You could see from the Mississippi River to Lake Pontchartrain from his corner office in the Hibernia Bank Building. Using his folksy demeanor and country twang as courtroom props, Ray had won ten million dollars for the families of three people who drowned when a cargo ship plowed over a passenger ferry carrying petrochemical workers and school children across the river in the early-morning fog. It was the most money ever awarded in the St. Charles District Court.

Mimi had heard that Ray was having an affair with the young associate who had helped him in the ferryboat case. New Orleans was such a small place. Mimi wondered if Tish knew.

"There she is, there's my bride," Ray said as Tish and Mimi came down the stairs. "You want to get me a *G* and *T*, honey?"

Knock it off, Mimi thought. It's not cute any more, you pint-sized philanderer.

Tish and Ray went into the dining room, where Lady Pamela was debating with Florence about which serving pieces to use. Inez was sitting in the wing chair next to the heater with a glass of wine. Mimi went past them, into the kitchen, where Jessica and her boyfriend and Tish's son Burton were eating doughnuts. She went into the pantry and found a bottle of cabernet and a corkscrew and opened the wine. Then she grabbed one of Inez's old coats from a hook by the door, wrapped it around herself, and went out the French doors to the backyard.

Hidden way back in the corner behind the ligustrum hedge, hanging low from the big live oak, was the swing Big Eddie had hung the summer she was ten. She sat down, took a sip and settled the wine bottle between her thighs. Then she pushed back gently.

Big Eddie. He had been waiting at her dorm when Beau drove her home after the formal, sitting on a sofa across from the dorm mother, drinking a cup of coffee. When she walked in and saw him, she'd been scared to death. But he had hugged her and said he was sorry about not walking her down the stairs at Tri Pi. Two months later, he'd walked her down the aisle at Holy Name of Jesus Church.

Then, on one of those April days when spring was still warm and breezy, not yet hot and humid, Big Eddie had gone to Ochsner to find out why he was tired all the time. They did some tests, and decided it was cancer. Liver, pancreas, everywhere. Little Eddie came home from Boston and when he and Mimi stood in their father's room at Ochsner, it occurred to Mimi that the Eddie in the bed wasn't the big one anymore.

Their father opened his eyes and looked at them. "Son," he said, "I want you to do me a favor." His voice was soft.

"Sure," Little Eddie said.

"This coffee they give you in here is weak piss. I want you to go to the Camellia Grill and tell Thomas I need a big cup to go. You remember where it is? You take the River Road to Carrollton . . . "

"I know, Dad." Little Eddie looked annoyed.

"Well get going, then. You need any money?"

"No, Dad, I got this."

"And don't let him load it up with milk or cream. I want chicory, black, you hear?"

"Chicory, black," Eddie repeated, as he walked out the door.

"You need me to do anything?" Mimi asked.

"Yes, ma'am, I do. Come over here and sit by me," Big Eddie patted the blanket near his knees. He hiked himself up on the pillows so that they were face to face. His arms coming out of the hospital gown were pale and sprouting tubes.

"You're a beautiful woman, Mimi girl," he said.

She smiled. "Oh, Dad..."

"No, let me finish. You're a beautiful woman, and you're a married woman. And you got to stop acting like you're still some coed prancing around, flirting with every man comes down the golf course, and doing God knows what else."

"I don't know what you're—"

"Listen to me. I'm not saying you did anything, I'm just saying you're looking like you might."

"I don't know who you've been talking to."

"Doesn't matter who I been talking to. I got eyes, and so does your husband."

"What are you talking about?"

Big Eddie sighed. "You are still my little girl, my sweet little girl, and I wish to God I hadn't've let your mother take over with you. She might've got you all prettied up, but you were a whole lot nicer," he stopped and lifted her chin to meet his eyes, "and, I believe, happier before." Big Eddie swatted at his wrist. "I tell you what, this damn IV line is the most itchiest, annoying thing in this whole setup."

Mimi stared at him. "I don't know what you're trying to imply, but you are wrong. Dead wrong."

Big Eddie took Mimi's hand. "Be that as it may. Now I don't have a hell of a lot of time left to set you straight. You can go around and do what you want with who you want in Bay St. Louis or at the club or wherever, and you might get away with it, and you might not. But either way, you are not going to be a happy person. That man you married is probably one of the more honorable men I've known in my life, and as long as he's a good husband to you and a good father to Teddy, you better damn well be a good wife. Do I make myself clear?"

Not too long after that, they'd followed the hearse carrying Big Eddie out to Metairie Cemetery. That was what your children did for you, Mimi thought. They buried you.

The breeze blew Mimi's hair and her nose began to feel cold. Without opening her eyes, she lifted the bottle, took a swig and started to play the swing game. How liberating it must be to rewrite your very existence. It was Mimi's favorite pastime, trying to imagine Technicolor while she lived in black and white.

The French doors opened and Jessica and the boyfriend came out, holding hands. From behind the ligustrum, Mimi watched as they crossed around to the side of the house, where they couldn't be seen from inside. They were both wearing blue jeans and denim work shirts. Jessica had a turtleneck sweater under hers, but the boy didn't. He looked cold. Jessica shook her head at something he said and her long brown hair blew into her face. She leaned her head against the house and smiled at him. He stood over her, resting his hand against the house next to her.

He was tall and skinny, with dirty blond hair and beautiful clear tan skin. If Mimi were Jessica looking up at him, she could see what color his eyes were and smell his maleness. He leaned his head close to her ear and said something that made her laugh. She said something back and he leaned down again and kissed her. His Texas hand was caressing her shirt.

A car pulled into the driveway and he stepped away from the house and Jessica. Mimi watched Beau and Teddy get out. Mimi knew she was lucky. Beau and she had been married for eighteen years. Teddy was a sweet boy, and Beau was the perfect father, reliable and loving and stern when he needed to be. Not a football hero, not a hotshot lawyer. Happy with his numbers. Happy with his family.

Mimi had tried her best to be a good wife. It was easier now than it had been in the early years. Once you hit middle age and put on a few pounds, you didn't get tempted so much. Still, it seemed like she'd spent her whole life trying to please first her mother, then Beau. When it started to make her angry, she'd pour herself a glass of wine.

Though it was only just past noon, the day was overcast and all the lights in the house were on. From between branches, Mimi could see Florence holding up the cover of the turkey pan while Lady Pamela poked at it with a long fork. Tish and Ray were leaning against the counter, drinks in hand. Beau held a bottle of Dixie. Mimi gulped the last of the wine, tossed the bottle into the ligustrum and walked slowly to the house.

In the kitchen, Mimi walked over and pecked Beau on the cheek. "Game on?" There was always some crucial contest in the SEC on Thanksgiving Day.

"Pregame," he said. "If it's going to be awhile till we eat, I might go in and watch." Beau looked tentatively at Lady Pamela.

"Oh, I don't know, go ahead, I don't think it's tender yet. What do you think, Florence?" Lady Pamela usually cooked turkeys till they sliced like sawdust. "I read that you can get some awful disease from poultry. Salmonella?"

Ray and Beau went to the den. While Florence and Lady Pamela wrestled the turkey back into the oven, Tish started taking rice and oyster stuffing and cranberry sauce to the table. Mimi opened another bottle of cabernet and filled a wine glass.

In the dining room, Inez was dozing in the wing chair that Leroy had equipped with rollers after she broke her hip. Tish and Mimi rolled her up to the end of the table. Lady Pamela was peeved about Inez getting her place, but there was no other place for the wing chair to fit.

Lady Pamela knew instinctively the proper seating arrangement for any dinner party, and she had put nametags in silver holders at each place. But the kids had rearranged the place cards. Jessica and the boyfriend were sitting next to each other, holding hands. Beau, Ray, Teddy, and Burton were at the far end of the table, where they could see the television set in the next room. The three remaining chairs were at Inez's end of the table. Tish lit the candles.

Florence held the door open while Lady Pamela made her entrance with the turkey and placed it in front of Ray. "I see we're seated informally," she said. "Shall we say the blessing?" After grace, Ray carved and loaded each plate with turkey. The other dishes were passed, and Florence went around with the gravy boat. Then Ray stood and tapped his knife on his wineglass.

"I'd like to propose a toast," he said. "Son?" Burton reached in his pocket and got out a piece of bread, which he tossed to his father. Everybody laughed except Lady Pamela and Mimi.

"No, seriously," he said, "I want to dedicate a few words to Lady Pamela, who has prepared this wonderful meal so we can give thanks for all our blessings, but most of all for our family." He looked at Burton again, and put out his hand. "Son, do you have my address?"

"Fifteen eleven Peniston Street," Burton chimed. Even Lady Pamela was smiling now. Did they rehearse this stuff? Ray sat down, looking smug.

Mimi stood. She raised her glass and looked straight at Ray. "I think we all should think about how thankful we are for our family, on Thanksgiving and every day," she said. Her mouth didn't seem able to keep up with her brain. She steadied herself against the table. The candles smelled like mothballs. "Because after all, it's the people who are closest to us, who we are the most intimate with, who we depend on the most, who we are most likely to hurt when we forget about how much we have to be thankful for."

She sat down and looked at Tish. Nobody said anything for a few seconds. "That's enough toasts," Beau said. "Let's eat."

Mimi took a bite of stuffing and in an instant she knew that little oyster wasn't going to swim peacefully in the cabernet lake of her stomach. She shoved back her chair and ran for the bathroom.

CHAPTER SIXTEEN

dreams

MIMI WAS DRIVING HOME by herself in the Volvo. Suddenly the car was on a pier and the pier was sinking into icy water. She had to get off the pier. She grabbed the steering wheel and pulled and pulled but she couldn't turn it. Finally she managed to steer the car onto a boat, but it was sinking too. The boat was still close to land so she yelled and shouted, but nobody answered her. The boat was headed toward an island full of people but nobody could see or hear her.

With a start, Mimi awoke in a room dark except for fluorescent clock hands. 12:25 a.m. Her head throbbed. The last thing she remembered was the white ceramic tile on the bathroom floor of her mother's house, cool and hard against her face. Now here she was, fully dressed and under the covers in her old room. Her mouth was dry and her head pounded.

When she opened the bedroom door, she could hear a man and woman talking. In her stocking feet, she slipped through the door and left it cracked open. She stood in the dark hallway and peered over the banister. The Mississippi lilt of Lou-Ann Rainey, Inez's night nurse, was unmistakable, though Mimi could only see the back of her head. Lou-Ann was leaning against the archway into the dining room. The man was standing close but not touching Lou-Ann. From upstairs all Mimi could see was a windbreaker over a plaid shirt, the last three buttons straining to meet across his paunch.

"Don't be so jumpy," he said. "Everybody's asleep." The man's raspy voice had the low, intimate quality of an obscene telephone call.

Lou-Ann tried to talk but his lips were on hers and while he kissed her, his hands moved down her back. They stopped against her buttocks and he spread his fingers open , pulling Lou-Ann against him and maneuvering her into the dining room.

Leaning her back against the corner of the wall, Mimi slid to the floor. She closed her eyes, thinking of the days when she had heard such urgency in a man's voice.

There was a crash in the dining room and the sound of shattering pottery. Mimi could see fronds of Boston fern. "Oh God," Lou-Ann said and then Mimi could hear laughing. Then she heard Lou-Ann's footsteps fade away and the door of the downstairs bathroom close. Mimi's right foot was asleep under her and the prickles ran up to her knee. She peeked around the corner and could see his face as he sat in Inez's wing chair, leaning back with his eyes closed. His gray hair was thinning and his skin was the kind of ruddy that either meant outdoor work or drinking too much. Mimi stretched her leg. The floorboard creaked.

"You can come out now."

Was he talking to her? Mimi's cheeks burned. She inched back into the shadow and held her breath. The grandfather clock on the landing chimed one. On her butt, Mimi scooted backward into the bedroom. She slipped on her loafers, stood, walked into the hall, and closed the bedroom door behind her. Ostentatiously. She walked as forcefully as she could into the hallway and down the stairs, putting her full body weight on each step. At the bottom, she looked away from the dining room and flipped on the hall light switch. Her heart pounded.

He stood up and put out his hand. "Harry Madere, a friend of Lou-Ann's. I was, ah, dropping her off for work." He smiled. Mimi took his hand. He squeezed hers and didn't let go. She couldn't speak and couldn't break away from his stare. Down the hall, the toilet flushed. Over his shoulder, Lady Pamela and the other debutantes, seated demurely with their ankles crossed, gazed down at Mimi. She pulled her hand back.

"Mimi Delery. Mrs. Percy is my grandmother. I came down for aspirin. How do you do?"

Harry smiled. "Fine. Very fine, in fact." He looked right into her eyes. "How are you?"

"Fine, thank you. I came down for some aspirin." Why was she explaining herself to him? She could feel herself blushing.

"Hi, Mrs. Delery," Lou-Ann said from the hallway. "I hope we didn't wake you up, us down here talking and all. And I accidentally knocked over this plant. I'll go clean it up right now."

"No, no, I just now woke up, just a minute ago. I was looking for some aspirin. I think there are some in the kitchen." She passed in front of Harry without looking at him. "Oh, and Lou-Ann, you probably should check on my grandmother."

Mimi got the pills from a kitchen cabinet, grabbed her coat and purse, and headed out for the swing. She sat for a moment so the cold air could clear her head. She closed her eyes tight.

On the street side of the ligustrum, a car door slammed and an ignition turned over, caught, and then killed. The ignition turned again, revved, finally caught. She listened to the motor hum. Then she reached in her pocket for her car keys and walked over to the Volvo, still in the driveway. When Harry screeched away, she pulled out behind him. He turned on Nashville Avenue and headed toward the river. There was a good amount of traffic but it was easy to follow Harry's Chrysler because one of the rear lights was out. He made a left at Magazine Street and pulled up in front of Rinse's Bar. Mimi drove a block beyond and pulled over. She looked in the rearview mirror. He was going into the bar.

She hadn't thought about Rinse's since some of Big Eddie's friends had gone there after the funeral. It was on the stretch of Magazine that had gone upscale in the last dozen years. Shops that used to sell used furniture now advertised "antiques." There were restaurants with patio seating, wine bars, gourmet food stores. But Rinse's was a remnant of the old Magazine. Its big plate glass window was hung with heavy velvet drapes to help the old Fedders built into the side wall keep the place cool. She wondered if it was the same inside. She thought of Beau, at home asleep.

No, not at home. At Ray's camp on Lake Maurepas, as always on Thanksgiving night. He and Teddy both. Out to the middle of the swamp. You could only get to it by boat. There were four sets of bunk beds, a kitchen and a bathroom that you wouldn't want to shower in without shoes on. Ray had bought it nine years ago and Mimi doubted it had ever been cleaned. There always was a big party, a guy thing, on Thanksgiving weekend, a couple of lawyer friends of Ray's, some of their clients. They brought their sons and if there weren't enough beds, the boys got sleeping bags. One year one of Ray's partners brought his daughter. He wasn't asked back.

They'd be gone till Sunday night.

Mimi got out, walked back a block, and opened the door to Rinse's Bar.

CHAPTER SEVENTEEN

awake

DOOR . . . WINDOW . . . MIRROR . . . SPARKLING river through blinds . . . bright lights . . . dim lights daytime nighttime. Where am I? I hate that feeling of waking up in an unfamiliar place. Let me think . . . Octavia . . . no. What a tacky little motel . . .still what did I expect? No . . . not Octavia. It's Causeway. . . headed back. Maybe you should drive. I finished off that bottle of wine . . . he's nodding . . . Oh well got to get gas in the Volvo . . . wait . . . no haze . . .fog tree bayou . . . loud loud headache . . . loud wet wet wet all over moving moving fireman . . . slits glass sparkles . . . hurts.

Hurts.

Clear drip drip. Bag connected to hose. Snakes down . . . who knows where . . . hurts.

Voice . . . deep smooth . . . soft. Thick thick ear carpet. Rub ear. Caress. Up down. Close far away.

* * * *

"Good morning, Mimi. Are you ready?"

Yes, yes, I'm ready. I've been waiting for you. It's you I want, Velvet. You talk softly to me, and not only when you tell me how the X-rays look and whether we should up the dosage or switch to another one or try to wake up. You always ask how I feel and you always listen to what I say. You hear. You understand.

"I thought I saw her blink, Doctor."

Hard floor. Linoleum? Outdoor carpet. Astroturf. Scratchy. Who is that? Why is he here?

"You can wait in the family room, Mr. Delery. Should be about six hours, once we get her in. You could leave . . ."

"No, I'll wait, in case she wakes up."

"All right—"

"It's okay. I know the drill. Don't get your hopes up."

* * * *

Good, Astroturf is gone. And I don't even care that horrible light is glaring into my eyes as long as I can still hear Velvet talking to me.

"All right, Mimi, I'll see you up in the OR. We're going to see if we can get that piece of glass in your head. Should come right out and then—well, then we'll see. Mrs. Benderson is going to cut your hair so we can get in there, okay? I'll talk to you after the procedure."

No, no. Don't touch me. Stop. Leave me alone. Stop that noise. It hurts. It hurts so much. Make her take that jackhammer off of my head. No. No. No. No. Stop it. No.

"All right, Mrs. Delery. We're going to move you onto this other bed and then we'll go up to surgery."

Stay away from me, Jackhammer. Don't touch me.

"Bill, can you come over on this side? You'll have to support her this way. No, don't let the arm go."

Stop it. Stop sticking pins in my arm. Stop it right now.

"Do you want to finish with the dressings before Dr. Kannemeyer comes in for the leg?"

"Let's wait on the leg. I think six hours is enough for her today."

You're back, Velvet. Don't let them hurt me any more.

"And it's not like she's going to be walking out of here."

"Nurse."

"Sorry, Doctor."

"You never know in a case like this what the patient hears."

"I know, Doctor. Sorry."

Thank you, Velvet. What is that smell? Is something burning?

* * * *

"It breaks my heart to see her like this."

"My God, Tish, what was she thinking?"

"She was thinking about drinking herself into oblivion."

"How could she do this to the family?"

"Shhhh, it's Teddy. Come on in, honey, it's only Gran and me. Look, doesn't she look better today? The doctor says she might come out of it when the swelling goes down after the surgery. Don't cry, Teddy. Don't cry."

Buzz, buzz, buzz. Where did all these wasps come from? Teddy, can you ask Daddy to get rid of that wasp nest? Teddy? Teddy? I'm talking to you, Teddy.

* * * *

"We got all the glass we could out of her skull and as far as we can tell, nothing went any deeper. We still have the trauma, though, and the brain swelling."

"Which means what, doctor? When the swelling goes down, will she—"

"It's only been a few weeks, Mr. Delery. Your wife was in a very serious accident. She's lucky to be alive."

"You call that lucky, Doctor? Look at her."

Shut up, Mother.

"Yes, Mrs. Percy, I call that lucky."

"Bottom line, Doctor. Will she come out of it?"

"That's hard to tell, Mrs. Percy. Every case—"

"Dr. Benjamin. We got you here because we were told you are the best neurosurgeon at Ochsner. You have the most experience with these things of anybody in New Orleans or in the South for that matter. You have seen this before. So tell us, will Mimi wake up? And if she does, will it be Mimi or some vegetable in the Poydras Home for the rest of her life?"

And what kind of a name is Lady Pamela anyway? You think you're some kind of royalty? Well you're not. You're just a snob, like your mother was too. Who names a baby Lady?

"All right then, bottom line. Your daughter has suffered cerebral hypoxia, a traumatic brain injury. For some period of time, we don't know how long, her brain was without oxygen. How severe the hypoxia was, is what we don't know. Her eyes, verbal, and motor responses are significantly lower than we would like at this point in her . . . recovery."

"How significantly?"

"We use the Glasgow Coma Scale to rank . . ."

"In English please."

" . . . to rank a patient's responses. Right now Mimi is a six on the scale of fourteen."

"And is it possible she will move up on that scale?"

"I will tell you exactly what I know. And that's that I have no way of knowing when she will get better. Or whether she will get better."

A dog owner. That's who names a baby Lady. You know what that makes you, Lady Pamela?

* * * *

"Mom, Notre Dame was awesome. You should see their stadium, Mom. There's this giant Jesus looking over it and they call him Touchdown Jesus. And everybody is really into it. I got to go to classes and spend the night in the dorm. And you should see the band, Mom. It's really cool to be in the band. Not like being on the football team, but still cool. They have this thing they call Drummers Circle. It's part of a concert before the game on Saturday but they also do it at midnight on Friday and everybody comes out. I mean everybody. All the students, and they're cheering. You play a riff and it's 'Go Irish go,' over and over. And 'Can't stop the Irish.' They do it on the xylophone too, like we did in jazz band. I'm really glad you and Mr. Witmer talked me into staying in band. I talked to the band director at Notre Dame about when the tryouts are and everything. I know you and Gran wanted me to go to Tulane and all but . . ."

Oh no, Sweetheart. Notre Dame would be wonderful. Teddy, I am so proud of you, my sweet, handsome boy.

"Dad, do you think she hears us?"

"I don't know."

I hear you, Teddy. I hear you. I hear you.

* * * *

"It's not 'pulling the plug,' Mr. Delery. It's weaning her off the ventilator to see if she can breathe on her own."

Tubes, tubes. Hiss hiss. Pale blue hose. Hiss hiss. Pleats, kinks. Hiss hiss. Mouth to hose. Hiss hiss. Neck to hose. Hiss hiss. Itches in throat. Hiss hiss. Gag.

"And what if she can't? Can we put her back on?"

"We would have a plan, surely. We would monitor what we call her rapid shallow breathing index to see if she is able, on her own, to respirate sufficiently and certainly, if not, the wall oxygen will—"

"So that means she—her brain—could be even more damaged, is what you're saying."

"Yes."

"And there's no way of telling how much damage there is."

"Not unless she wakes up."

But I am awake. I'm here, Beau. I'm here. I'm fine. Look at me, Beau. I'm so sorry. But I'm fine. Touch me. Hold my hand. Look at me.

CHAPTER EIGHTEEN

bastard

"CAN I TELL YOU something about the suit without you getting mad at me?" Emmaline settled into the vinyl and steel barstool at Rinse's and yanked her skirt down.

"Me mad?" Peg said. "You're the one who had to hand those idiots at EEOC the sex discrimination case they've been looking for all these years. And you're supposed to be my friend."

"It's not about you," Emmaline said. "It's about those arrogant assholes who run the newspaper, on Howard Avenue and in New Jersey. Have you seen the payroll records we subpoenaed? Did you know that even though there are five female reporters with more than ten years' experience, not one of them is paid as much as the lowest paid male reporter just out of school? And not one woman ever got a signing bonus at all, much less the ten grand they gave to that DeForest guy out of Princeton who's all of twenty-three years old."

"That was moving expenses," Peg said. "Plus he was talking to *The New York Times*."

"You can't even say that with a straight face."

They sat in silence for a few minutes, waiting for the bartender to move their way. Emmaline sighed. "Look, I'm not blaming you for doing your job and being on their side."

"Unlike your cohorts."

"Okay, we probably need to not talk about this if we're going to stay friends." Emmaline shifted in her seat, trying to straddle a large crack in the vinyl. "Don't you ever get tired of this place? I have to get a new pair of pantyhose every time I come here."

"Don't bitch so much," Peg said. The bartender finally looked at them and Peg signaled for two beers. "You always want real. Well, this is real. This is the real New Orleans, not all that tourist stuff in the Quarter."

"I may have said authentic. I didn't say decrepit. I mean, look at this place. They keep it so dark because even the creeps who hang out here couldn't stand to see what it looks like in the light of day."

Peg laughed. "The last time I was here with Gabe, we were sitting right about here. I'm looking in the mirror and out of the corner of my eye I see something crawl out and before I can say anything, the bartender pulls a paper towel off the roll and slams it down on the counter. 'Was that a roach?' I asked him. 'What?' he says. 'I'm just keeping the counter clean.'"

"Couldn't you have waited till we were leaving to tell me that?"

The door blew open and gusts of rain blew in, along with a man holding a trenchcoat over his head. Peg waved at him. Beau Delery stamped his feet by the door, shook himself out of his raincoat and rolled it up as he walked to the bar. He hugged Peg, then Emmaline, leaving both of them wet.

"I'm not sure that raincoat helped you much," Emmaline said.

Beau looked down at his sopping clothes. "Sorry," he said. Peg moved over to make room for Beau between her and Emmaline.

"How are you?" Peg asked.

"Good, good. Teddy and I, we . . ." Beau stopped and waved for a beer. "We went over to see her after dinner, we always do when he comes home. Then I dropped Teddy off at his friend's house."

"How's Teddy doing?"

"He loves it in South Bend. He didn't get in till this morning because they grounded the planes out of Chicago yesterday with the snowstorm. So we were late to Thanksgiving dinner."

Beau shook his head. "You know the strangest thing? I checked the visitors' log at the nursing home going back two months, and Lady Pamela hasn't been there once. We go to her house, and nobody even talks about Mimi. Her own daughter. I think she wishes Mimi would just disappear." Beau looked down at his drink and his shoulders heaved. "A year now. A whole year. I don't know what I'd do without you two to talk to."

Peg touched Beau's arm.

"You remember back at LSU?" he said. "I knew she was drinking too much. But we all were back then. And then we had Teddy, and she left school, and I don't know, I just looked the other way." His shoulders slumped and he rubbed his eyes. "And if I'd been there instead of at that stupid camp, I'd have been driving. . ."

"It's not your fault, Beau," Peg said.

They sat silently. Finally Beau looked up. "She was so full of life. *Is.*"

"What does the doctor say?" Emmaline asked.

"He says there's no change."

"What do you think?"

"I used to think her eyes lit up when Teddy came in. I used to think I could feel her squeeze, just the tiniest bit, when I held her hand. Not lately." Beau looked first at Peg, then Emmaline. "But the nurses say all the patients have good days and bad days."

Emmaline waved to the bartender. "I think I'm going to get a rum and Coke, you all want anything?" Peg and Beau shook their heads. The tables at Rinse's had filled with a Thanksgiving night crowd, people leaving other people's houses and not ready to face their own yet. But except for them and a man on the end stool in the corner, the bar was empty. As she took her drink, Emmaline looked into the mirror and her eyes met the man's. They held for a moment. Then he looked down, and Emmaline turned back to Beau. "Did you and Mimi ever talk about, you know, if one of you . . ."

"No," Beau said. "We never did. The doctor asked me that, too. But I know she wouldn't want to be like this. I just have to be sure, really sure that she can't, that she isn't . . . Look, I better go. I need to pick up Teddy."

"I'm ready too," Peg said.

At the door, Beau got his umbrella and offered to walk them to their cars. "Go ahead," Emmaline said. "I have to go to the bathroom."

After Peg and Beau left, Emmaline went back to the bar and sat down next to her brother Harry. They both looked into the shadowy mirror behind the rows of bottles. "Rum and Coke?" Harry asked her reflection. Emmaline nodded.

She'd always known this day would come.

* * * *

The decades evaporated, and she was hitchhiking home after visiting Bonnie at the lakefront house. A car pulled over and she didn't realize till she opened the passenger door that the driver was her own brother.

As she climbed into the front seat, they had both laughed at their audacity, her for being out so late and alone, Harry for taking Merle's car.

The house was dark as they pulled into the driveway, but they could see blue images from the television through the living room window. It was turned up so loud that they could hear Johnny Carson as soon as they got out of the car.

Ruby was sleeping on the sofa. Emmaline turned off the TV and in the sudden silence they heard whimpering from the back bedroom. Emmaline felt her heart sink into her stomach. "No!" she yelled and ran down the hallway, Harry behind her.

When she opened the door, she saw Merle on the bed with Jolene.

"You bastard," she said.

"Take the baby out," Harry said.

"He's not going to get away with it this time," Emmaline said.

"Take Jolene out of here," Harry said. Jolene was sucking her thumb and crying, her thin legs splayed. Emmaline gathered her sister's arms up, wrapped them over her shoulder and lifted her. Jolene's head rolled around, her eyes unfocused.

"Did you give her something?"

"Just a little whiskey, loosen her up," Merle said.

Emmaline lunged for him, but Harry pushed her and Jolene aside. Already husky and tall at fifteen, Harry picked Merle up under the arms and pulled him out to the backyard. Merle cowered, his hands cupped over his privates.

After she'd dressed Jolene in her pajamas and tucked her into bed, Emmaline looked out the back window. The yard was empty. Emmaline went to the closet and took a bundle down from the top shelf. Then she opened the back door.

Outside was pitch black. The streetlights didn't reach to the end of their yard, much less into the Weeds. There wasn't a lighted window in any house on this side of the block. As she got closer, Emmaline could hear slaps and punches. It was nearly midnight, but so hot she could feel sweat trickling down her back. She walked into a clearing, where somebody's father had mowed a baseball diamond. As her eyes adjusted, she could see Harry's back. Merle was on his side in the grass, his skinny nakedness curled up into a ball.

Harry turned to her. "He won't be a problem anymore," Harry said. "He's going to leave tonight and never come back. Ain't you, Merle?" Harry stuck his toe under Merle's chest and flipped him. Merle's face was bloody.

Merle lifted his head and opened his mouth. A tooth dropped out. "You jealous, are you, boy? Well, you can have this one here, but not the other. She's my sweet baby girl."

The shotgun blast knocked Emmaline backward. She stood and walked close enough to see that Merle wasn't smiling any more.

"Why'd you do that?" Harry look scared. "Somebody's going to call the cops."

* * * *

They worked as quickly as they could. They got the shovel from the carport and dug into the soft loamy earth by the canal. It lifted easily, but the hole kept filling with water. They gave up when it was two feet deep. Emmaline brought a blanket from the house and they dragged Merle down to the hole. Then they threw wet sewer dirt on Merle and his shotgun.

* * * *

Now, Emmaline turned to the brother she hadn't seen in decades. That last time, Harry was pulling out of the driveway in Merle's car. Emmaline had gone back inside and climbed into bed next to Jolene. She hadn't been able to get to sleep, wondering if the police were going to knock on their door.

Harry raised his glass and nodded. Then he reached over and put his arm around her shoulders. Emmaline lay her head against him, feeling warm and safe.

CHAPTER NINETEEN

coma lady

THEY FILTERED OUT FROM breakfast, some slow and stooped, others hot-rodding on late model scooters. Or power-walking. Some joked with the nurse pushing the med-trolley as she handed them their morning cocktails of pills in little paper cups, then poured second paper cups of water. They gulped the pills and then tossed back the water chaser like a shot of smooth bourbon. Others were more careful. One lady stirred the pill cup with a crooked bony finger and said one was missing. Seemed to be accusing the nurse of deliberately shorting her.

"No, Marie," the nurse smiled. "Remember, Doctor said you don't take the orange one anymore." But Marie didn't remember.

Some of them stopped along the hallway and collapsed onto strategically placed armchairs, gasping for breath from the effort of traveling ten feet. He watched one woman get from the breakfast room to the front parlor—maybe ten yards—going from armchair to armchair, stopping for forty-five seconds or a minute at each before moving forward a few feet to the next chair.

Maybe thirty years, if that much, between him and them. In less time than from his first job mucking stables at the old Jefferson Downs to now, he would be shuffling from chair to chair, from bed to grave.

"You see that?" An old man sitting near him motioned to the newspaper on the coffee table. He turned to see who the old man was talking to. Nobody else was within earshot.

"I'm waiting for somebody," he said. But then realized that the old man didn't care why he was there. Just wanted to talk.

"He lives here," the old man continued. "Or did. Used to be a professor at LSU."

"Who?"

"Him, the one in the picture. They couldn't recognize him, but the police came here 'cause of the car registration. So we knew it was Miller, even before we saw his Saints cap sticking out of the car."

He looked at the paper, where the old man was pointing. There was a blurred photograph of a mangled car surrounded by firemen with hoses pointed at it.

"Left after lunch, went out there to LSU, said he had papers to grade. Damn fool been retired for years. Wanders around awhile, talks to some professors, probably bothers the secretaries. Does that once or twice a week. They know him, humor him. Kind of. So this time, he stays till after dark, you know. Cop says he must've been confused, turned the wrong way onto Airline Highway. Eighteen-wheeler guy didn't even see him.

"Here for lunch, gone before dinner, room cleaned out by breakfast. You never know." The old man shook his head. He folded his hands in his lap, pursed his lips. A low-pitched reverberation osmosed out of his throat. "Oomph oomph."

They sat in silence for a moment. He wanted to escape, but he had no idea where to go, and the nurse who told him to wait had disappeared.

"Oomph oomph." The old man shook his head again, then put out his hand. "Emil Engqvist," he said.

"Harry . . . Morris."

Engqvist's grip was firm but brief. None of that new-fangled two-handed stuff.

"Guess you can tell I'm Swedish. Father was, anyway."

Harry hadn't given it a thought.

"Father came over in Ought Three, knew some people from Malmo, the D'Arensbourgs. They had come over and settled up on the German Coast, St Charles Parish. You ever heard of them?"

"Lots of D'Arensbourgs around," Harry said.

"Yeah, well, my daddy comes to Louisiana, goes to Des Allemands where the Swedes were. Meets my mama up there. Her daddy was a fisherman. He does that for a while after they get married. But there's not too much money in fishing unless you got your own boat, and my granddaddy had three sons fishing with him already. Then Daddy hears about these jobs in the copper mines, out in Arizona. So that's where they move. Got three kids by then, me and my two brothers. All five of us, out to Arizona. Oomph oomph."

He paused, shook his head, looked down at his fingernails. Took out a crumpled handkerchief, blew his nose loudly. "My mama said it was good in the beginning, lots of money, nice house, you look outside and all you see is mountains, all around. Real pretty."

"What happened?" Harry asked.

"Daddy died. Mama left there with seven kids, my oldest brother twelve. Mama had to come home to Des Allemands, which is where we all growed up."

"Was it a mining accident?"

"No, more's the pity. Then we could've gotten some kind of pension from the company, Mama said. It was internal bleeding, his appendix burst, and they had to take him down from the mountain in a horse buggy, eight hours to get to the hospital. Thirty-seven years old."

The nurse came up behind him, putting her hand on his shoulder. "Mr. Morris? You can see Mrs. Delery now."

Harry got up. Emil Engqvist stood too. "You here for the coma lady?"

"Um, yeah, I used to know . . . her family."

"Real shame, that is. In the beginning, there used to be a few people come to see her, family mostly. How's that son of hers?"

Harry put his hand out. "Nice talking to you, Mr. Engqvist."

"Emil. Yeah, see you around."

Harry followed the nurse down the hallway. The place was clean, antiseptic smelling, but underneath, something else, something stale. An old woman in a robe and slippers stood perfectly still in the hallway, holding onto the wooden handrail, looking straight ahead. The nurse didn't seem to notice her.

At the end of the hall, the nurse opened a door and went in. Harry stayed at the door. The bed was on the far side of the room, near the window, and the lump in it was turned toward the window. The room was dim, and all Harry could see was the back of a head of gray hair, cut very short. As he got closer, he could see that the lump was curled tight, knees up to its chest. The hands were clenched into fists.

The nurse went to the window and adjusted the blinds. With the burst of light, so intense that it made Harry squint, he could see her eyes, and they were open. But even though the sun hit her full in the face, she didn't stir. Not even an eyelash.

"Mimi, you have a visitor," the nurse said. "Harry is here. Do you remember Harry?"

Not a movement, not a blink.

"Where did you know her from, Mr. Morris?'

"Why?"

"Well, maybe we could talk about that, remind her. Oh, well, it doesn't matter." She straightened the top sheet and blanket, bustled around the room. "Come over here so she can see you."

He stepped forward slowly. Her face was thin, yellow. She looked as old as the woman in the hallway, though Harry knew she was younger than he was.

The nurse moved to the door. "Talk to her," the nurse said. "You never know what she hears."

He sat in the chair by the window. Thought back to that night. He probably should have been paying better attention, but she had fallen asleep and her head was going forward and he'd let go of the steering wheel to reach over and try to grab her shoulder so she didn't hit the dash and then he'd had to swerve for the other car.

Once they crashed, he had no compunctions about getting the hell out of Dodge. It wouldn't have made a bit of difference if he had stayed. She had already been thrown from the car; there was no way he could have helped her. Probably would have made her worse if he'd tried.

And there were too many people looking for him.

And it wasn't like she needed that money in her purse.

If she'd been sober, she would've been driving and none of this would've happened. So it was really her fault.

Though he'd had a few too. And maybe he should have tried harder to buckle her seatbelt before they started. But wasn't everybody responsible for themselves?

Still, he felt real bad when Lou-Ann talked about it. Seeing the husband with Emmaline made it worse.

Why did he even leave Rinse's with her? That was the real pisser.

Lou-Ann thought they ought to allow her to die in peace, not have her hooked up to machines. She was breathing but not living, Lou-Ann said, a thing not a person. But the husband wouldn't allow it.

Lou-Ann didn't know Harry had been with Mimi that night. Nobody did, he guessed. Nobody knew but him and God, and so far neither one of them had been able to figure out why. He should have walked out of Rinse's alone that night. That's what a decent person would have done.

Now, all he could think about was this woman, curled up and hooked to tubes. Staring at nothing.

He'd asked Lou-Ann if it was that simple. Just pull a plug? Not quite, she'd said. But almost. She'd known a nurse who she suspected had stepped on a cord, but the family didn't pursue it. Lou-Ann thought they were relieved.

Harry looked at the tube snaking from her arm to the drip bag, and the other one in her neck with the big open hole. Such little connections to life. One electrical short, one blocked passage, and it's all over.

He got up and walked to the back of the machine, all the while watching her face. Waiting for a movement, a twitch, a blink.

Nothing.

He reached over, did what he came to do, and left, closing the door softly. He could hear a faint, persistent beep as he walked down the hall. Emil Engqvist waved to him from the sitting area.

CHAPTER TWENTY

discrimination

"WILL YOU BE NEEDING a cab, miss?" the redcap asked as he grabbed Peg's suitcase off the carousel.

"Yes, please, downtown."

He waved down a cab and Peg handed him a five as he loaded the suitcase into the trunk. She hated having to rush back here after the New England trip. Another round of recruiting interviews, but for once she'd arranged it so that she would have time to see a play in New York before flying back. Until this stupid trial got pushed forward and Marv Steiner, the *Item*'s lawyer, told her to get back pronto.

The cabbie waited for the light to turn on Airline.

"Don't go the interstate," Peg told him. "Airline to Tulane is quicker."

She tried to think through what was likely to happen today. She might not be called to testify, but Marv (whom Peg thought of as Mr. Belt and Suspenders) had decreed that she had to be here and ready, in case Fred Cronin said something so awful that the plaintiffs decided to quit while they were ahead. He'd said things in closed meetings and at parties that would end the case immediately and probably cause Marv himself to write out a check to the EEOC. But Fred was a pretty cool customer. Peg didn't think he would slip on the stand.

Airline Highway was depressing, with its rusted railroad tracks and used furniture stores and motels with Coke machines next to the front door. No wonder the Tourist and Convention Bureau tried to route tourists out of Moisant toward the interstate. But to Peg, it was almost like looking at someone you love who isn't pretty anymore, or even presentable, an old broad whose lumps and wrinkles were magnified with the shortened breath and clogged arteries of having lived too well for too long. But do you stop loving her?

In almost no time, they pulled up to the Hale Boggs Federal Building, huge and modern, with its concrete courtyard fronting six lanes of Poydras Street. Peg signed a cab charge slip with the *Item*'s account number for the airport ride, and a second one for the driver to take her suitcase to the newspaper office.

The wide hallway was silent and cold, even though it was eighty degrees outside. Peg sat on a bench outside the courtroom, as Marv had instructed. It felt strange waiting outside the court, when all the action was inside. When she was a reporter, she was always inside, or running around looking for an attorney for a quote. Now she was the boss, so she waited outside, while the action inside the courtoom was about the newspaper. Staring down at the veins in the marble floor. Waiting to be called as the next witness in the *United States of America, Equal Employment Opportunity Commission vs. The Times-Item Publishing Corporation.*

Exhibit A for the defense. The managing editor, in charge of the whole newsroom. How could anybody say the *Item* discriminates against women?

The big door to the courtroom opened and Randy Boudreaux, the *Item*'s federal court reporter, came out. Peg waved. "Recess?"

"Nah. They let the jury out for a few minutes while the lawyers wrangle so I thought I'd grab a smoke."

"How's Fred doing? Oh, wait, I guess you're not supposed to tell me."

Randy laughed. "Yeah, the last thing we need is more co-conspirators."

Conspirators. Like there was some big plan to all this. Like Fred and Lawson sat up at night planning how to discriminate against women and blacks. That part, at least, was ridiculous. They didn't have to plan. It came naturally. Maybe it was in the water, big bottles of additives that Sewerage and Water Board workers dribble in like snowball syrup at the Carrollton intake on the Mississippi River.

Gabe was on the witness list. Peg tried to remember how much she had told him about their jokes about the reporter who was pregnant, the intern with the short skirt. Fred had talked openly. Almost like he had forgotten Peg was in the room. Was he so confident in her? Had Fred bought her silence with promotions and raises? She tried to focus on her testimony but couldn't stop thinking about Gabe.

They had been heading north on the Airline Highway toward Natchez, Peg driving, when Gabe told her about his time in the Irish Republican Army. The beauty of the Irish countryside. Being able to move about freely because he was American, and using that freedom to help the republicans against the RUC. Going to the post office to pick up the shipment. Hiding the guns. Holding up a bank to get money. For what? More guns? Bombs? Gabe paused. "That was ten years ago," he said.

"Did you kill anyone?" It was only four in the afternoon, but the winter sky was already streaked purple.

"Not then."

The traffic was suddenly heavy, quitting time outside one of the Baton Rouge refineries. *Was all this IRA stuff true or another of Gabe's stories?* Peg had begun to think he didn't know the difference. The road was clogged with pickup trucks with gun racks in the cab and vinyl liners in the back. They passed a pickup with three large men in hardhats inside. "When?" she asked.

"I don't want to talk about it," he said.

And now she would see him again, for the first time since he was fired from the *Item*.

Peg had nothing to do with his expense reports; they all went through the sports department. But that didn't excuse her. To Gabe, she was a collaborator. One of the Vichy French, co-opted into the Uptown Nazi Establishment. And he was one of the oppressed, the victims, despised for his lower-middle-classness. He reveled in Establishment contempt, and could recount any number of examples of his persecution. Like the time after a high school football game between Jesuit and Holy Cross. Gabe had been on the Holy Cross team, and some girls at the game invited Gabe and his friends to a party at Valencia, the Uptown teenagers' club. Before the first dance was over, the Holy Cross boys had been tapped on the shoulder and informed that Valencia was for members only and they'd have to leave. The boys walked the three blocks back to St. Charles Avenue and were waiting for the streetcar when Gabe decided to go back. He picked up a big rock from a front yard and lobbed it through Valencia's front window.

That was Gabe. As soon as you start to sympathize with him, he made you sorry.

A bailiff came out and propped the courtroom doors open. People filed out. Peg could hear Emmaline before she saw her.

"Come on," Emmaline said. "Let's go eat."

* * * *

It started to sprinkle so they ran across Poydras to the grimy brick building that housed Mother's Restaurant. Two men in business suits and two others in T-shirts, jeans, and hard hats stood on the sidewalk under the overhang, smoking. The line stretched outside the double doors at the entrance, and they huddled forward, trying to stay dry.

Once they were finally inside, Peg pointed to the red beans, and a thin black man wearing a white apron put three ice cream scoops of rice on a plastic plate then ladled smoky, fragrant beans and sauce over it. There were hunks of pork, and the thin juices quickly saturated the rice and formed a dark red moat around the edge of her plate.

They paid at the cash register, took their trays to the end of one of the long tables, and sat across from each other. "How was the trip?" Emmaline asked.

"Good, I talked to some good prospects. Lots of women and minorities, you can tell your buddies at EEOC."

"Okay, let's not be a smart ass," Emmaline frowned. "Have you heard from Gabe?"

"No," Peg said. She broke off a piece of pork with her fork, "Mary said he all but called me a liar in his deposition."

"Now that's rich." Emmaline took a sip of ice tea. "That man wouldn't know the truth if it arrived at the Superdome on an Endymion float. You know he used to go up to Angola once a month to see Rock? Franky says they're very tight." Emmaline wiped red gravy off her chin with a paper napkin. "It's just not right to eat this stuff without a Dixie."

"We could order a couple."

"What, and go back and have to face Marv? Are you trying to set up the opposition, honey?"

"I did a story on the state prison once, and I visited Angola," Peg said. "It seemed so, I don't know, remote. Scary. They say people try to escape by swimming across the river, but the bodies always wash ashore in a week or so. Do they still make the inmates grow sugarcane?"

Emmaline mopped up a last bit of pork with a slice of French bread.

"He's out."

"What? I thought he got fifteen years."

"Good behavior."

"Wow, he must have changed."

"He told Franky he found Jesus. Also that it's my fault he's in prison."

"He always was delusional."

Emmaline looked down and pushed a grain of rice with her fork.

"No, actually he's not." The rice continued its slow circumnavigation of Emmaline's plate. "Sometimes you do things you think you should, but you shouldn't, even if it's for a good reason. And sometimes you get so angry, you do things you know you shouldn't."

"Are we still talking about Rock?"

"That day Rock left and drove down to Cocodrie, you remember he told the cops he got a phone call?"

"Yeah, you said he thought it was the bait shop guy's wife, what was her name?"

"Bergeron, Sandra Bergeron," Emmaline said. "Rock's lawyer tried to get her phone records. But it wasn't her." Emmaline looked at Peg. "It was me."

"I kind of figured that."

"I almost told you, that first night when you brought me home after the deputies came."

"What difference does it make who called him? He's still the one who shot two people in cold blood."

"His lawyer told him it would have been mitigating, if they could've proved the call was from somebody trying to set Rock up, or, or. . ."

Emmaline looked out the window of Mother's. The gutters were barely holding back the cascades of rain from the line of people still waiting to get inside.

"I was just so angry," she said. "He had left, yet another time. Left me, left Franky when I had to go to work. But I just wanted to hurt him, I never thought he would do that. Never."

CHAPTER TWENTY-ONE

witness

"AND ON THAT TUESDAY, August 9, was there a meeting in the office of editor Fred Cronin?"

Peg paused, took a breath, looked at Jane Grovius, the EEOC attorney. "There was a meeting in his office every day."

"If I tell you that notes in Mr. Cronin's office calendar, maintained by his secretary Mrs. Alicia Rubio, reflected a meeting on that date at eleven o'clock in the morning, and also lists you as one of four people in the office . . . Excuse me, Madam Clerk, may I have Plaintiff's Number 15?"

The clerk rummaged through stacks of exhibits while Grovius waited. Her grayish brown hair looked like it had been cut around a bowl on her head. Her suit was black, her blouse white, her shoes plain and low-heeled. Free of any vestige of makeup or lipstick, she could be a nun.

"Thank you, Madam Clerk." Grovius picked up a small binder calendar, walked over to the witness stand and handed it to Peg.

"Please turn to the ninth of August."

Peg flipped through the pages.

"Read me the entries for that date."

"Seven a.m., breakfast mayor's office. Nine-thirty, production meeting, second floor. Eleven, new hires, editorial. Noon—"

"Thank you. Now please read the entry on the other side of the page."

"New hires meeting: Personnel, notified; suburban editor, notified; Hennessy, notified."

"Thank you, Ms. Hennessy. Now do you remember the meeting?"

"We had many meetings like that on many different days." Peg looked at Marv. He shook his head a millimeter, reminding Peg that she mustn't let Grovius get to her. She must appear open, friendly.

Grovius took the calendar back to the plaintiffs' table and looked at some notes. The courtroom was packed with people, but most of them seemed bored by the endless recitations of memos and dates. Even Emmaline was doodling on the paper in front of her.

"If I told you, Ms. Hennessy, that the meeting was called to discuss the hiring of Janet Gilligan, would that help you remember the meeting?"

"Yes."

The door at the back of the courtroom opened. Rock Thibaut came in and stood against the back wall. A bailiff motioned him to a seat at the middle of the next-to-last row. Rock edged in, stepping over legs and feet.

Grovius picked up a deposition and leafed through it.

"I have here a description of some of the conversation at that very meeting, as related by you to a third party within a day or so after the meeting. I would like you to read from this document."

Rock was still edging over people in the back of the courtroom, finally coming to an empty seat next to the wall. An elderly woman looked annoyed as she lifted a canvas bag off the seat to let Rock sit. She leaned forward and wobbled as she tried to stand and balance the bag. Before she could fall over sideways, Gabe jumped up from the row behind and caught her.

"Your honor, I am handing the witness the deposition of one Gabriel O'Malley, former reporter at the *Times-Item* newspaper."

Peg took the booklet. Her face was burning. Her neck and ears throbbed.

"Ms. Hennessy?"

"Yes?"

"Please read from the point on Page 28 that I have marked."

Peg looked down. The type seemed to swirl. She took a deep breath.

"Question. Did Ms. Hennessy recount to you information about a meeting in which news executives discussed a female candidate for the job of River Parishes bureau chief?

"Answer. Yes.

"Question. What did she say?

"Mr. Steiner. Objection. Who are we talking about?

"Ms. Grovius. Sorry. Who was the prospective employee who was being discussed?

"Answer. Janet Gilligan.

"Question. What did Ms. Hennessy tell you was said about Janet Gilligan?

"Answer. Well, first you have to understand that before they brought her in, they knew from her application that she had two kids who were, I don't know, pretty young. What they didn't know until she showed up was that she was pregnant.

"Question. Okay.

"Answer. So Peg walks into the meeting, and Fred and Lawson and the other guy, I think it was Steve Anniston, were laughing. So Peg sits down and says, what's so funny?"

The courtroom was quiet. To Peg, it felt surreal, reading her own words twice removed. She coughed.

"Do you need some water, Ms. Hennessy?" Grovius asked. Peg shook her head. "Then please continue."

Peg looked down at the booklet. How long would she have to go on? She took a breath and started reading again: "So Fred says, well, you have to understand, they knew about two kids, so this chick shows up for the interview looking like she's ready to, well, looking very pregnant. In fact, they were afraid they might have to drive her to the hospital instead of out to the bureau. But anyway, she gets through the interviews, goes back home. So it's the next day and these guys are talking about whether she would be good for the job. And Peg comes in and they're all laughing pretty hard, so Peg says what's so funny. Fred says, we were wondering how we can find out whether she's going to keep popping them out every year."

There was a titter in the courtroom.

"Please continue, Ms. Hennessy."

Aha. Suddenly I see where this is going. Coffin ready, nail poised, here I go.

"So Peg says, Fred I don't think you can ask about stuff like that."

"That's enough, thank you, Ms. Hennessy."

Grovius is having trouble keeping her mouth out of a smirk.

"Now do you remember the meeting?" Grovius asked.

Peg looked straight at Grovius, not at the defense table, not at Marv. No point in equivocation now. "Yes," she said.

"And were those your words?"

"More or less."

"Okay, more? Less? Which is it?"

"Those were my words."

"Thank you. Now can you tell me what you meant when you told Mr. Cronin that he couldn't ask that?"

"That our Human Relations Department had told us—"

"That's the department that oversees hiring, correct?"

"Yes. The director had told us that we weren't supposed, that we couldn't ask about, couldn't ask questions to a woman, for example, that we wouldn't ask a man."

"And why was that?"

"Because the lawyers said we could be . . . we shouldn't."

"They said it was against the law, didn't they?"

Marv Steiner stood up. "Objection, leading."

"Sorry, your honor. One last question, Ms. Hennessy. To your knowledge, was there ever an instance when a male job candidate was questioned, or had comments made, about how many children he had, or planned to have?"

"No."

Peg looked at the plaintiff's table. Emmaline and the others were smiling. Grovius flipped through her legal pad.

"Ms. Grovius, do you have any more questions?" Judge Joffrey was known for being impatient.

"No, your honor."

Of course she doesn't. She's just pausing to let that sink in to the jury.

Grovius walked back to the plaintiffs' table. Very slowly.

Even before she was seated, the judge looked at the defense table, signaling Marv's turn to question Peg. Marv had told Peg that he didn't anticipate any problems, but if there were, he assured her, he'd easily be able "rehabilitate" her.

So get up and rehabilitate, Marv.

But the *Times-Item* lawyer wasn't watching Peg or listening to the judge. He had turned to the bench behind him, and holding his legal pad, was having a whispered conversation with Lawson Richardson, the paper's publisher.

Judge Joffrey was getting irritated. "Mr. Steiner?"

Marv stood up, holding his legal pad. "Your honor, I would like to request a recess. My clients are prepared to discuss a settlement."

Emmaline and her co-plantiffs hugged. Grovius' smirk widened to an actual smile. The *Item* had always said they'd never settle. Peg looked at Marv, who shrugged.

The judge banged his gavel. "We will reconvene at five this afternoon," he said.

"All rise," the bailiff called out as the judge got up. The reporters in the front row didn't even wait for Joffrey to get into his chambers before sprinting for the door. The TV stations would probably send live crews for their six o'clock news. Most of the spectators were filing out.

Peg stepped down from the witness chair and walked over to the defense table. "Am I done for?" she asked Marv.

He turned to see if Fred and Lawson were nearby, but they had already gone. "I didn't say this, right?" Peg nodded. "Your job is probably safer than Fred's right now," he said. "No way will they get away with punishing their only female executive because she told the truth on the witness stand."

Marv handed some papers to his assistant, who was loading boxes of evidence onto a dolly. "That being said, they might be justified in hoping that in the future, she'll be more circumspect, even in her private conversations."

As Peg started to leave, Emmaline broke away from the horde at the plaintiffs' table. "I wish it had been anybody else in the world up there but you," she said.

"Me too," Peg said. "But I'll be fine. Come on, let's go have that drink."

They walked out together, down the wide marble hallways where a few stragglers from the courtroom remained, into the elevator.

Outside, the rain had stopped. The plaza smelled steamy. News vans from Channel Four and Channel Six were parked on the sidewalk. The camera crews rushed toward Emmaline. She had beaten the Establishment. This was her moment.

That's why I'm backing away, not just so Lawson and Fred won't see me on the evening news.

From the back of the crowd of television reporters, Gabe looked at her and winked. He'd avenged his firing, for sure. This would cost the *Item* way more than the meals and hotel bills he had padded onto his expense reports. Next to him, Rock pushed forward.

Seeing them together makes me uneasy. For barely a second, I'm not sure why. Then it hits me.

"Emmaline!" Peg shouted.

Emmaline looked toward Peg just as Rock pointed his gun. There were screams and shoves as he fired. The marshals ran forward from the entrance, drawing their guns. People dropped to the ground or ran away. Another shot, then another.

I crawl toward Emmaline. Her leg is twisted at a strange angle and blood gushes from her neck. Her hand twitches. I push down on the hole in Emmaline's throat and feel the warm stickiness of life drain from her. She seems to want to say something, but she can't.

People were still on the ground. Crouching, the marshals slowly moved toward Rock, their guns pointed.

"He's dead!" one of them called out.

The air is smoky. I kiss Emmaline's forehead and think of weeds and cigarettes and willow leaves swaying in the heat. And of little truths that can be far, far worse than large lies.

Acknowledgements

As a newspaper editor, I have seen what writing looks like before skillful editing, and I know that writers often are loath to let go of their precious words and phrases. Joe Coccaro and Ellie Maas Davis were the best of editors: deft and discerning questioners of meaning and intent, skillful slayers of verbosity. Shari Stauch has been a coach, cheerleader and friend. I owe a great debt also to Sheila Grissett, Dawn Ruth Wilson, Ellen Bremenstul, Thomas Reeks, Joe Winter, Phil Arno and Eugene Blossman—all early readers, critics and improvers. Rosemary James and Joe DeSalvo gave me the nudge to get going. To the Mystery Book Club and the Middlesex Book Club—thank you, all of you, ladies and Dave—for being twenty-first century literary salons, islands of thought and conversation amid the rough seas of social media. AMDG.

.

THANKSGIVING
READER QUESTIONS

1. Several pivotal chapters in the book happen on or around the Thanksgiving holiday. Years after the opening chapters in the summer of 1965, we first get a good glimpse of Harry around the Thanksgiving opening of the Fairgrounds Racetrack. Emmaline visits her sister Bonnie in Houston over Thanksgiving, and goes to see her mother in the nursing home soon after. Middle-aged and alcoholic Mimi goes back to her childhood home on Thanksgiving,. After years of separation, Emmaline encounters her brother Harry on Thanksgiving. How do these events provide a theme for *Thanksgiving*?

2. What do you think of the different family dynamics— Mimi's, Peg's, and Emmaline's and Harry's—in *Thanksgiving*?

3. Who was responsible for the papers going missing in the Thanksgiving Day horse race, resulting in Harry's bet paying off? Could it have been just an oversight?

4. If Emmaline's family moved into a suburban neighborhood today, would neighbors or authorities

react any differently? Would Merle have been able to disappear without a trace?

5. What about Professor Miller? Could his 1970s behavior happen on a college campus today?

6. Do you trust Harry? With women (Lou-Ann, Mimi)? With money (racetrack incident, Mimi's purse after the accident)?

7. If Rock had fought in the Iraq War instead of the Vietnam War, would he have been diagnosed with post-traumatic stress disorder?

8. Who is your favorite character, and why? Is this the character you most identify with?

9. Who is your least favorite character? Was there any justification to explain the things that character did that made you dislike him or her? Does he or she have any redeeming social value?

10. Who is the better father—Big Eddie or Beau? Who is the better husband?

11. Other than "Daddy," we never learn the name of Peg's father. But we know Peg's mother is Mary Frances. Is the author signaling who had more influence on Peg's life?

12. What do you think of Mimi and Beau's marriage? What about Peg's parents' marriage? What about Rock and Emmaline's?

13. What parent or parental figure most influenced each main character—Peg, Emmaline, Harry and Mimi— for better or worse?

14. Three characters change names. Peg becomes Maggie, Frank Thibaut becomes Rock, Harry Madere becomes Harry Morris. What were the motivations for the changes? What did each get out of the new name/new persona?

15. Did clothing serve a symbolic purpose in *Thanksgiving*? Lady Pamela, in her bathing suit, leans too closely over the doctor examining her daughter.

Peg wears her white high school graduation dress to her first day of college. Then she wears blue at the Tri Pi formal, while all the sorority girls are in white. Mimi eagerly describes her fancy wedding dress made of French lace. And later, Mimi anticipates her mother's disapproval of Mimi's middle-aged dowdiness. Emmaline is climbing a rig in a miniskirt when she meets Rock.

16. Do the four main characters change in the 30-plus years *Thanksgiving* covers? How? Who changes most?

17. What role, if any, does religion—Catholicism—play in *Thanksgiving*?

18. New Orleans is a city of neighborhoods and neighborhood bars. Rinse's is a continuous presence for all the characters in the novel. How does each experience it differently—Peg and Mimi in childhood as well as later, Harry and Emmaline as adults?

19. Whose crimes are worse—Emmaline's (born of passion and anger), Harry's (calculated, thought out, but humane), or Rock's (born of anger and revenge)?

20. What did you think of the ending? Was it in character for Mimi? Harry? Emmaline? Peg?

CPSIA information can be obtained at www.ICGtesting.com
Printed in the USA
LVOW11s0004140116

470476LV00005B/683/P